THE SILENT WORLD

Around the world there was total silence from Pole to Pole. Seas crashed noiselessly on rocky shores, hurricanes shrieked mutely across the China Sea. People shouted and were not heard; alarms and bells rang and yet were mute. The dead wall of silence was everywhere — the most strident sound was unable to break through it. Scientists were unprepared for The Silence. There was something amiss with the laws which governed sound — but that was only the beginning . . .

JOHN RUSSELL FEARN

THE SILENT WORLD

Complete and Unabridged

LINFORD
Leicester

First published in Great Britain

First Linford Edition
published 2011

British Library CIP Data

Fearn, John Russell, *1908 – 1960.*
    The silent world. - - (Linford mystery library)
    1. Large type books.
    2. Science fiction.
    I. Title II. Series
    823.9'12–dc22

ISBN 978–1–44480–533–8

Published by
F. A. Thorpe (Publishing)
Anstey, Leicestershire

Set by Words & Graphics Ltd.
Anstey, Leicestershire
Printed and bound in Great Britain by
T. J. International Ltd., Padstow, Cornwall

This book is printed on acid-free paper

1

The silent world

There was a 'something' in the air — indefinable and yet subtly forcing itself upon the attention. It was somehow similar to the sensation produced before a violent thunderstorm. The summer air crawled with it. The soft, hot breeze was supercharged with it, and yet there was no visible evidence to account for it.

Very few people concerned themselves in any case. They went about their daily work, or pleasure, without heeding the strange, prickly sensation that was affecting every exposed portion of skin. Most people assumed it was 'sunburn', for the summer of 2019 was unbearably hot, particularly in the metropolis. Others wondered if it were some mysterious form of skin disease — and still others just didn't care anyhow. They were in the majority.

The scientists cared, though. It was their duty to keep the populace informed of the cause of unexpected happenings; but in this instance they were baffled. All the national physical research laboratories went to work with their highly developed instruments, but they could not entirely account for the prickly irritation affecting every human being. It certainly did not appear to be the work of the sun — despite the fact that it developed a sudden severe rash of sunspots — for the effect was present night and day.

Something in the atmosphere then? Possibly; but nothing showed up on the instruments. Then it dawned on one group of scientists that they were perhaps looking too close to home for the solution. Perhaps it lay out in space itself, and Earth was swimming through the midst of it?

So the giant telescopes and various other instruments used for spatial analysis were put in action for this specific purpose and earnest men and women the world over gazed out into the deeps and did not at all like, or even partly understand, what they detected out there. They did not *see* it in the accepted sense of the word, but the instruments revealed its presence.

'Never been anything like it in the natural form before,' declared Elmer T. Walters, the great American physicist.

'Definitely dangerous!' pronounced Hertz, of Europe.

'Something that formerly has existed only as a theory in the minds of great electrical wizards is now revealed as a fact — and a dangerous one!'

This last was the statement of Holt Rankin, the forty-year old chief of the astronomical physics division in Britain.

The cause of the trouble was known by mid-August and the scientists of the world gathered in London to discuss the matter behind closed doors. They had looked upon the onset of something that was so alarming they could none of them trust themselves to theorise upon the startling consequences that might follow. Certainly the heads of the world's governments had got to be secretly informed, but as yet the public was best kept in ignorance so as to avoid panic,

'Do you believe,' asked Elmer T. Walters, as the conference progressed, 'that we have a manifestation out in space of a genuine dyno-depressant?'

'No doubt of it!' Hertz of Europe sat back in his chair and stared complacently through dense spectacles.

'I estimate it to be a hundred million miles beyond the orbit of Pluto,' observed Henri Tourlaine, the French mathematician. 'And therefore already in the Solar System.'

'Correct,' agreed Holt Rankin, the Englishman. He was tall, bony, with the sombre eyes of a thinker and the jaw of a doer. 'And because it *is* a dyno-depressant we have no means of forecasting exactly what it will do. We know, however, that it will certainly affect electrical waves, and maybe other waves as well. Since at the moment it is in the region of the outer planets, and advancing steadily this way, we do know *one* thing: it is not affecting light-waves, otherwise we would not be able to see the region of space where it lies. That, perhaps, is one

4

blessing . . . But there are so many things it *can* do,' he finished moodily.

After a long silence the American physicist slapped his hand on the table.

'One thing is certain, ladies and gentlemen, we cannot just tell the public that a dyno-depressant is in space and likely to involve the whole Solar System, including Earth and Sun, for the simple reason that no layman would know what a dyno-depressant is. We hardly know ourselves, for that matter, and what little knowledge we have of such a condition only serves to heighten our fear of the consequences. How this thing ever came to develop we may never know, and as far as we can tell, with our woefully imperfect instruments, the extent of the field may be tremendous. Definitely we cannot see its further limit, which means it could stretch right outside the Solar System beyond known limits.'

'Quite possible,' Hertz agreed. 'And it will be constantly growing, drawing unto itself the energies dispensed from the stars and background cosmic radiation. It is a grim situation.'

Finally a scientific report was drafted to the satisfaction of every delegate present and facsimile copies of it were promptly transmitted to the head of every state and country in the world. Each ruler, man or woman, read the statement privately and realised that something was going to happen to Earth that had never happened before. The report did not necessarily imply the end of the world, but it *did* envisage a disturbance that would affect all electrical waves and vibrations. Anything *could* happen, but no scientist was willing to take it upon himself to say what.

In general, science assumed that some fourteen days would see the dyno-depressant enveloping the Earth, and then whatever was going to happen, would. It was recommended that the men and women of the world be kept in ignorance not only to prevent possible panic but also because it could not be definitely stated what was going to happen. Since vagueness was no use, silence was best.

There were, of course, a privileged few

who had warning that something untoward, if not unpleasant, was likely to happen within fourteen days — and these privileged ones were the relatives of the scientists who could be trusted to keep the information to themselves.

Linda Rankin, Holt's wife, was one of the few. In his usual brusque way Holt gave her the details, forgetting that since she was not a scientist she had hardly any idea of what he was talking about.

'Dyno-depressant?' she repeated, spreading her hands. 'What in the world is that? Sounds like an illness.'

'It is,' Holt agreed moodily, his sombre eyes upon her. 'An illness of electricity and energy — or if not that then an abnormal form thereof.'

Linda shrugged. 'It won't interfere with our holidays, will it?'

'It will interfere with everything, Lin! It's not even possible to say with any certainty that we'll even be alive in two weeks' time.'

Linda was silent, puzzling things out to herself. She was a slim, chestnut-headed girl, formerly a secretary in the physical laboratory of which her husband was now the chief. But her inclinations were not scientific. They were domestic — and the delightful home they possessed on the outskirts of London was her main interest, eclipsed only of course by her devotion to the terse, lanky man who, for all his abrupt manner, worshipped her.

'You mean,' Linda asked at length, uncoiling from the chesterfield where she had been sprawled at ease, 'that things are as bad as all that? Because of the dyno-whatsit?'

'Yes.' Holt rose to his feet from the hassock upon which he had been squatting with the inelegance of a schoolboy.

He wandered to the open French windows and gazed through them on to the riotous flower garden, then beyond to the misty warmth of the summer evening. There was the distant sound of children laughing in the nearby recreation ground — and more remotely still the excited barking of a dog.

'Hear that?' Holt asked briefly, as Linda wandered to his side and put an arm about his waist.

'What? The dog?'

'Uh-huh. It's got the prickles, same as you and I have. Same as everybody has. The dyno-depressant is causing that. It isn't a dangerous condition, mind you, but it makes animals excited because they haven't the emotional control of a human being. Summed up, it's electrostatic energy.'

'Oh!' Linda said, and smiled. 'Just as long as we know — but what a lovely evening,' she added, sighing. 'Calm and warm. Been a lovely summer altogether,'

'Let us enjoy it whilst we may,' Holt muttered.

Linda's hand crept from his waist to his arm. There was a vague look of fear in her brown eyes now. She had never seen her husband in such a mood as this: he was harassed, embittered, and even hopeless, whereas he usually found something redeeming in the darkest situation.

'Holt, you've said a lot and yet haven't told anything. Because you know what you're talking about you assume everybody else does. But they don't you see.

Certainly not me. Just what is all the trouble about? What's coming?'

He turned, whipped up two cushions from the nearby armchair and tossed them on the step.

'Sit,' he instructed. 'I'll do my best to explain.'

Linda obeyed and he settled beside her, bony knees upthrust. 'It's like this, Lin . . . There has developed in space something that, so far, has only existed as a theory in the minds of the most advanced thinkers in physics. This 'something' is technically referred to as a 'dyno-depressant', the first half of the word being derived from 'dynamics' and the second half referring to a dampening field of energy, which, for want of a better phrase, is called a 'depressant'. Stated simply, a dyno-depressant is a form of electrical energy which is neither positive nor negative and therefore outside our knowledge. In scientific circles it is called a bastard energy — '

Linda nodded, her whole attention on the subject. Holt was satisfied she had followed so far, and continued:

10

'Michael Faraday, one of the most advanced electrical thinkers, believed that there was an electrical energy in existence outside of the familiar positive and negative on which our whole electrical knowledge is based. He could only postulate upon it, but never brought it into being. After his day several other physicists and scientists of note underlined his statement and this theoretical bastard energy, glimpsed occasionally by experts in electrical experiments, was given the name of 'dyno-depressant'. I'm not sure if it were not Soddy, another great physicist, who did the christening.

'The point is this, Linda. By some process which we have not the knowledge to understand, there has appeared in space a vast field of electrical energy which is neither positive nor negative as we know it, which does not produce a reaction on standard equipment, but which does betray itself on highly sensitive detectors as a form of electrical energy producing an intensely dampening field on all normal electrical waves. That means it must be a dyno-depressant of vast dimensions, created perhaps by cosmic energies, by some flaw in what we consider is normal electrical behaviour — The fact remains the entire Solar System is swimming into this area of unclassified energy and the results are unpredictable.'

'Why so?' Linda questioned, hugging her knees.

'Because just as negative and positive energies have their own particular laws — such as like charges repelling and opposite charges attracting — so this bastard form of energy also has its laws, and we don't know one of them! It is obvious though that it will be bound to affect both our positive and negative energies and that will inevitably mean chaos — '

'Such as lights going out and power going off, you mean?'

'Far, far greater possibilities than that, Lin! To realise just what it can mean you have to remember that every material object is electrical in basis due to the fact that it is atomic in construction. Electrical energy is the root of everything, and with that root disturbed by an unknown form of energy we can't say what *will* happen. We might disintegrate. On the other hand living tissue might not be affected at all but some other form of electric energy. The prickly feeling that everybody is experiencing at the moment is caused by the onward advance of the bastard field. Just as you get a 'hair-raising' effect near a powerful dynamo, due to its electrical emanations, so there is a similar effect here as the thin, outer perimeter of the bastard field advances.'

'Then what's going to happen when we're squarely in the midst of it?'

'We don't know.' Holt shook his head dubiously. 'My own guess is that the effect will become no worse upon us personally because the alien energy will have so many other forms of electricity to affect. It is the disastrous consequences to what we call 'normal' electricity that are so alarming. If anything goes seriously wrong with that all civilization can come to a standstill.'

'Oh, I don't know,' Linda mused. 'After all, civilization, of sorts, worked all right before the discovery of electricity.'

Holt smiled gauntly. 'Poor old Linda! You don't get the point. You picture electricity as the electric bulb, the radiator, or the television. You forget that you yourself are positive and negative electricity also. You can be destroyed in an instant of time. So can I. Everybody! Or, if it takes a different aspect and attacks inorganic objects, the ground and all known things could dissolve into some new form of energy. All theoretical, Lin, I admit, but terrifying just the same.'

'And it's all due to happen in a fortnight?'

'As near as can be estimated.'

Linda was silent for a moment or two and then she gave a smile. 'Oh, well, all in the day's work! We'll cross the bridge when we come to it.'

Holt smiled too, but moodily. He was thinking at that moment how truly ignorance can be bliss and wishing he himself did not know so many grim possibilities . . .

For all that he did not make any further reference to the matter in the days that

14

followed. He had his normal work to pursue for one thing; and for another there were no apparent changes in everyday life to claim his attention. The 'prickles' were still present certainly, but neither worse nor better than they had ever been, so all that could be done was wait and see what happened.

As for the public in general, there was no sign of disturbance because no warning had been given. It meant nothing to the average man and woman to tear off the calendar days, quite unaware that each day brought matters nearer a crisis.

On July 10th, the day fixed by the scientists for the coming of the 'D-D', as the profession now universally called it, Holt would dearly have loved to absent himself and stay with his wife, but in his position it was quite impossible. Every moment of his time was demanded at the physical laboratory, mainly to supervise the army of scientific workers who were standing by with apparatus to examine the first effects of the intruding electrical field. So Linda was left to herself and so unscientific was she, and so absorbed in matters domestic, she had quite forgotten it was *the* Day — until towards eleven-thirty a curious happening reminded her.

She realised suddenly, in the midst of dusting the lounge, that she no longer had the 'prickles'. To suddenly find herself entirely free of that irritating tickle on every exposed portion of flesh was such a surprise she could hardly believe it for a moment. Then she remembered. July 10th! Something had happened, and she was free of a physical annoyance that she had begun to accept as an inevitable part of living. Not that she was alone in her emancipation. All over the world, at about the same time, the 'prickles' stopped as mysterious changes of energy took place in the electrical fields spanning the Earth in multifarious forms. A mighty octopus of unclassified electricity was thrusting its tentacles into the midst of normal energies and forcing them to follow unpredictable paths.

In the physical laboratories the most notable thing to be observed to commence with was the wide deflection of compass needles from the magnetic north and also an abrupt increase in the area of sunspots — a fact reported by static-blurred radio from Mount Wilson.

Linda was so delighted that she started singing to herself as she continued her household duties. The idea of ringing up Holt and telling him what had happened occurred to her; then as she realised how busy he must be she refrained.

Instead she switched on the radio to keep herself company, but to her annoyance the music was nearly blasted out of existence by the sizzle of 'frying egg' interference.

'Oh, what's the use?' Linda demanded, fiddling with the volume control. 'Just when I want to — '

For some reason the last part of her sentence did not escape her. She knew she said ' — enjoy myself this has to happen!' but she neither heard it or 'felt' it within her throat. And at the same time the noisy radio muted down into silence.

'Now what?' Linda demanded — but again no words came from her. There was only the mental impulse, otherwise she might as well have been dumb.

Her hand trembled a little on the volume control. The radio was utterly quiet, and it remained so even when she turned the volume control to maximum. It was as though the power were off — yet it was not. The pilot light was glowing brightly.

Not only the radio was quiet: everything was quiet. Linda released the knob at last and turned slowly, looking about her. The sun was shining brightly through the French windows as before. Everything was cheerful and warm — yet quiet. Outside, for the windows were open to cool the room, there were no sounds whatever.

Fear suddenly had Linda in its merciless grip! She let herself go by screaming once at the top of her voice, but, though her breath expelled violently there was not a trace of sound. So that was it. She was stone deaf!

Shaking with fright she half-tumbled to the window and looked outside. The flower garden looked as it had always looked, but the normal rumble of daily life and the inevitable sounds from the nearby recreation ground were absent. A great aching quiet was on the world.

Fixedly Linda watched a lark soar suddenly from the meadow beyond the garden. Presumably that bird was trilling to its heart's content in the hot sunshine, yet there was no trace of silver song. Not the faintest whisper . . .

Linda screwed her fingers in her ears and twisted ruthlessly, even to the point of hurting herself, but it failed to make sound apparent. Still in the same state of anguished confusion she hurried from the lounge, knocking over a pedestal and flowers on the way. Both hit the polished woodwork around the carpet but neither made any noise.

Ignoring them Linda raced into the hall, wrenched open the front door, then raced down the sunny pathway to the gate. Here she stood staring dumbly at the usual stream of traffic passing the house. Only this time it was a soundless stream and drivers were looking puzzled and harassed.

Quiet. Deadly quiet. Everywhere.

Even as she considered the traffic

Linda realised that some of the drivers were pulling sharply at their cars, and this fact gave her a sudden sense of relief. It seemed that others too were mysteriously deaf: that it was not an affliction that had abruptly come to her alone.

Altogether, the traffic was proceeding as usual, since none of it relied on actual sound for its progress — except in the matter of horn-blowing. Possibly even horns were being blown, but there was no sound from them, nor from the car engines — nor from anything else . . . Linda looked up and around her. The sky was calm the sun warm. Nothing wrong up there. Nothing wrong anywhere except this uncanny mausoleum stillness. From force of habit she made up her mind to ring up Holt right away, then even as she reached the front door again with soundless footsteps she appreciated that telephoning was right out.

What, then? Bewildered and troubled she returned into the lounge, quite unaware that millions of people were just as bewildered as she was by the sudden failure of sound.

Apparently the 'fault' had involved the whole world.

There was a blanket of total silence from Pole to Pole. Seas crashed noiselessly on rocky shores; hurricanes shrieked mutely across the China Sea. People shouted and were not heard; alarms and bells rang and yet were mute. The dead wall was everywhere and not the faintest whisper or the loudest shout was capable of breaking through it.

And the scientists? Being only human beings, despite the elevated knowledge provided by their profession, they were as scared as everybody else. The Silence had caught them quite unprepared, too, but at least they knew it was not a physical affliction that had descended upon them but something amiss with the laws responsible for sound.

As the hours went by and the Silence showed no sign of lifting a deluge of enquiries began to pour into the various scientific organizations — all of them in the form of e-mails or telephone text messages. To answer them individually was impossible, so what information could be given appeared in the early editions of the newspapers, or as written words on the television, all normal programmes now being suspended.

For the first time the story of the encroaching dyno-depressant appeared, and hardly a single man or woman understood it. Instead there was the danger of panic. Buried in utter silence, their voices and ears useless, men and women could not be blamed for the terror that was overcoming them. It made it worse when nobody could speak to them directly by radio or telephone, when only the printed word made sense.

It was towards nine-thirty on that amazing summer evening when Holt Rankin returned home. Somewhat to his surprise he found that Linda had kept her head well enough to prepare a meal as usual, even though she looked white and scared as she came out into the hall to greet him.

She said nothing, knowing it was useless, but her arms went quickly round his waist, He gave his tired smile and hugged her shoulders gently, speaking a few soundless words. Then he jerked his head towards the lounge, through the open doorway of which he could see the laid meal.

Crossing to the bureau he wrote a brief note: 'Take it easy, Lin. Nothing to get scared of. I'll freshen up and explain later what has happened.'

Linda read the note and nodded, looking a little more cheerful now Holt was beside her. She had implicit faith in him and his scientific knowledge. She would no longer have to fight the Silence alone.

Holt washed, then returned downstairs, to tackle his meal hungrily, even though the knife and fork made no sound on the plate and he and Linda were enveloped in stony quiet. They kept glancing at each other, conveying their meaning by signals as far as possible, and so got awkwardly through the meal. This done, Holt switched on the standard lamp to mitigate the twilight, and then settled down on the chesterfield with a notepad on his knee. Linda drifted across and sat down beside him. Holt scribbled hurriedly for a long while and then handed across the sheet of paper. Linda read:

'The failure of sound is directly caused by the dyno-depressant. I said its effects would be unpredictable, and this is one of them. Sound, technically explained, is a vibration in the air, the differing wave-lengths producing different sounds. The dyno-depressant, in which Earth is now completely enveloped (together with most of the Solar System, as far as we can tell) is preventing the normal molecular vibration of the air which produces sound, so everything has become silent and will remain so indefinitely.'

Linda picked up the pad after a glance at her husband's serious face, swiftly pencilled a question:

'How long do you mean by indefinitely? As a scientist you must have some idea when the business is going to pass away?'

'No idea at all. We cannot locate the limits of the dyno-depressant. Naturally the occurrence has brought chaos, and will bring even more. It means that we have to write everything, use sign language, or else lip-read. Those with

24

mobile phones or computers can use texting or e-mail of course, but this may not last if radio and other electromagnetic waves become affected. Mankind has had many afflictions hurled upon him, but none so universal or so tragic as this.'

Linda could not find it in her heart to write anything further. Even though the total deafness which had closed upon her was not her own personal tragedy, but one shared by everybody on the face of the Earth — including animals — she could not rid herself of the feeling that she was alone and shut out from something whereas everybody else was normal. For a moment or two she even cried, then Holt's arm went about her shoulder again whilst he wrote with his right hand:

'Don't take it to heart too much, dearest. Man is the most adaptable of animals and there'll be a way round this. Science will discover ways and means to bring sound back again: have no fear of that. In the meantime, we all have to grin and bear it. Maybe it would help if we started to practise lip-reading!'

Linda nodded eagerly, glad of the chance to take her mind off the all-embracing quiet. So she and Holt began their first experiment in lip-reading, checking their results in writing. On the whole, knowing each other so intimately, they made good progress, with a silent laugh here and there in between as they completely misinterpreted a word.

But not all men and women were able to be so philosophical, or so practical. There were those to whom sound was life, and one such was Madame Emma Barconi, the great Italian prima donna. That her real name was Judith Soames and that she was born in Peckham, was nobody's business but her own. The fact remained that Madame Barconi faced a desperate situation. She had before her a line-up of concerts for the autumn and winter season that were extremely lucrative — yet now she was faced with this! Total silence

She had been practising in her London hotel suite when sound had ceased around eleven-thirty that morning, leaving her with her mouth wide open, her arms outflung, and her stupendous bosom expanded to the limit. Like everybody else she had assumed at first that she had been stricken deaf and dumb. Now she had read the newspapers she knew the effect was universal. For some it meant the possibility of groping along somehow until science found a way to defeat the problem; but for her it was extinction. She lived for her art, and with her amazing voice utterly stilled she was doomed. Such was the musically one-track mind of Madame Barconi it never occurred to her to try some other form of employment, or even to retire altogether on her already overstuffed bank account.

No; she must assume that this was her personal tragedy. Already her London manager had been — and gone. His exchange of notes had confessed his bitter regrets, but what was the use of a singer who could not be heard? All he could do was implement the contractual clause of 'Act of God' and call the whole thing off.

So Madame Barconi completed the personal tragedy that evening and threw herself from her hotel window, a distance of seventy-five feet, to the London thoroughfare outside — and by so doing she started an epidemic of suicides amongst those to whom sound was the breath of life.

In the days that followed the newspapers were full of accounts of those for whom the unabated Silence had proven too much. Orchestra leaders, composers, singers: these were the first to go. Not all of them committed suicide: some were strong-willed enough to resist this first impulse and instead changed their occupation to the already overcrowded ranks where sound was not essential.

Hardest hit of all were those in the theatrical profession. Every theatre in the world closed down automatically. The whole acting profession vanished overnight as it were, with actors, actresses, producers, sponsors, and all the ragtag and bobtail of the profession in the discard. Close behind them came the cinemas. From the lordly, glittering first-run houses in the heart of London, to the smallest back street talkie house, there came the same tale of woe and extinction. No use whatever in films that could not be heard.

No use? Samuel T. Glotzenhimer of Hollywood, who was in London when the Silence descended, was one optimist in the midst of the worldwide chaos. Until the Silence he had controlled seventeen great studios, all of them making handsome profits. In one night he had seen the lot swept out of existence — maybe forever, unless the Silence lifted. But did he jump from his hotel window or push his bald head into the nearest gas oven? No! Samuel T. was a man of opportunity, and in the universal quiet he made his 'voice' heard with reams of paper.

He would produce silent pictures! Yes, he would return to the rip-roaring days when the sub-title made the picture and the gestures of the players were fascinating to behold.

Samuel T. stood like a beacon light to the thousands of the acting profession who had been made derelict. They could be used: the films could be televised. There was a fortune in it. It was, to

Samuel T., a case of silence being golden.

If sound came back — all well and good.

He was prepared, when in Rome, to live as the Romans do.

Other optimists were the paper manufacturers, who saw in the worldwide calamity a chance to cash in. The demand for writing and printing paper had never been so tremendous — and the sagacious businessmen went to work to feed the Moloch. Their prices were adjusted accordingly, and certain paper tycoons saw the opportunity of netting a fortune out of a world's dilemma — until several governments stepped in and created a 'ceiling', which acted as a damper on these enthusiastic gentlemen.

By and large humanity adjusted itself amazingly well, chiefly on account of mobile phones and the internet. Young people found themselves besieged by parents and grandparents — who had previously disparaged the practice — to tutor them in sending and receiving text messages, Those people who did not have a personal computer rushed to rectify their omission, and to get connected to the internet in order to be able to communicate with distant friends and relatives via e-mail.

The days came and went, and there was not a ghost of a sound in the silent world. The only ones who were not the least concerned by this disaster were the deaf-and-dumb ones, and it was to them that the officials for public welfare turned in the hope of gathering a few hints to alleviate the desperate position.

A conference was called in London, to which delegates of all countries were invited to attend, the chief item on the agenda being a discussion to bring into being a universal sign language to take the place of normal speech. In a word, mankind had to start all over again to learn to develop non-mechanical means of how to keep in contact with his fellow man.

Strange, desperate days, with the stolid Western world slowly adjusting itself — or trying to — and the Eastern pagan world indulging in an orgy of religious fanaticism, believing the affliction was the wrath of the gods. The outstanding fact was that almost everything had to be re-learned from a different standard, since nearly every occupation relies on sound for its correct performance. Airmen in particular, accustomed to radio for directions and safe flight, had to alter their methods and rely entirely on visual instruments. Gradually, in every walk of life, as week succeeded week and the Silence showed no sign of disappearing, visual aids took precedence over the former audible methods, and in the background was the great shift and confluence of men and women changing their occupations and trying to fit into jobs already overcrowded.

Strikes, riots, panics . . . they slowly became more numerous, and in particular the governments of the world were vilified for not having given warning of this tragedy. What were the scientists doing, anyway? Apparently they had been asleep before the disaster, and apparently they were asleep now! Certainly no information seemed to be forthcoming from them.

2

Revolt of the women

In truth, however, the scientists were working to the limit of their ability. They were not magicians, even though some people considered they ought to be, and they could only draw their conclusions from their instruments. Depressing conclusions they were too. It was revealed now as incontrovertible fact that the dyno-depressant field extended for millions of miles beyond the Earth in the direction of the sun; whilst in the opposite direction, out towards the orbits of the giant planets and the limits of the Solar System, its depth was incalculable. Presumably, by now, the whole System was involved barring Venus, Mercury, and the sun itself. And they too would inevitably be involved in due course.

Added to this the scientists had the difficulty of being unable to speak to each other. Everything had either to be written down — for an immediate colleague — or in the case of a long distance, mobile phone texting or e-mails had to be used.

And, so far, the scientists could hold out no measure of hope. For all they could tell the D-D might be infinite in extent: it might even involve a complete change in the actual material structure of the Universe. Because positive and negative had always been assumed to be the basic energies of the Universe there was no reason why the law could not change — as indeed it had, chaotically.

Since the scientists refused to commit themselves, principally because they did not know what to say, the public made its own demands felt through the news-papers. What about space travel? Since something had made the Earth a silent planet, why not fly into space and escape the misery? To one of the other worlds? Patiently it was pointed out that (a) space travel was as yet a hazard inadequately developed; and (b) it would not do any good anyway since every planet was in a similar predicament . . . and with this the general public had to be content.

Eventually the selfish and the passive ones warred with each other, the aggressive ones elbowing the quieter types out of the way. And all of it done in silence, or else by the new sign language which was rapidly being acquired in all parts of the world. Indeed it was compulsory to learn it. Holt Rankin and his colleagues had learned it, and with Holt there was the added advantage of the lip-reading he was slowly perfecting.

'As far as we can see, boys,' he 'said' one morning, speaking with his fingers whilst his colleagues watched, 'there is nothing to be gained by continuing probing with our instruments. The D-D has us licked, and because it is of a class of energy about which we know virtually nothing we cannot possibly predict what it will do next, or when its hold over normal electrical fields will relax — if ever. For some reason sound particles have been utterly dampened, and that seems to the limit, so far. If new horrors are to descend upon us we'll have to accept them as they come. Our time would best be devoted to developing instruments for more careful analysis of D-D, and also to evolving scientific methods by which our voices can be heard despite the absence of normal sound waves.'

'How, for instance?' one of the men signalled.

'I'm thinking of a refinement of the audiophone employed by astronauts in spacesuits. Radio, actually, used for communication in the vacuum of space where there are no sound waves anyway. We might see what we can get out of that idea. I believe Luther, who designed the suits for the European Space Agency, has produced some quite novel ideas.'

So Luther, one of Europe's leading scientists, was immediately sent for, and in collusion with Holt, went to work on the design of a simple yet effective apparatus which, when complete, should enable the voice to be heard despite the breakdown in sound waves. This was to be Mankind's first answer to the deadly challenge of the dyno-depressant that had perhaps not yet even begun to exert its full malignant influence.

In the few brief intervals he took from his work Holt was aware of the deepening confusion settling upon the mute Earth. There was, for instance, the major problem of the children. All schools had had to be reorganised to read everything by sight only — yet, as the harassed Minister of Education pointed out, what was the use of teaching children about the everyday world if perhaps throughout their lifetime it would remain eternally silent? The youngsters were being set off on the wrong course from the very beginning as their parents were quick to see.

Once again: what were the *scientists* doing? Could they say how long this appalling state of affairs was to last? If for all time, then why not say so and let everything be planned that way? If, in time, the Silence was likely to lift, then it meant that no basic change in education was necessary. To this continual demand the scientists were compelled to answer — and a grim answer it was, made by Holt Rankin himself.

The Silence would last indefinitely, possibly for generations, since there was no measurable limit to the field of dyno-depressant energy through which the System was passing. He had not wanted to make this statement, but public clamour had permitted him no alternative; and, as he had expected, Mankind in general was again bitter in its condemnation of the men who had failed to sound a warning note.

Finally, wearied with weeks of gruelling work, including the planning of the 'radisound' apparatus which was now half-completed on the drafting board, Holt applied for — and was granted — a weekly vacation. He felt he had to have it or else go stark crazy.

The weather, fortunately, was kind. Up to now the D-D had not produced any appreciable effect on the electrical currents which, at root, are responsible for climatic conditions — so Holt and Linda took advantage of the Indian summer and spent most of their time outside, wandering through the silent fields, doing their best to enjoy picnics, yet always with that deadly feeling of having become isolated from the world they had once known. How long had it been now? Six weeks? No, eight and a half weeks had gone by since that ghastly morning when sound had gone from the world, perhaps forever.

Holt was perhaps the more acclimatised of the two to the changed conditions. He had mastered lip reading and sign language, the two essentials to his work, and the silence of everything else did not trouble him because he spent much of his time thinking and disliked disturbances. But to Linda, never given to much introspection, the reaction was entirely different.

The wind stirred over the long, late summer grass, and there was no answering rustle from a myriad dry blades rubbing against each other. The wind was heard no more in high telegraph wires and pylons. The trees made no sound as they bent gently against invisible, noiseless pressure. The insects were mute; the birds flew and no longer sang. The cattle were silent. A distant train climbed laboriously up a gradient, but the noise and clank of its effort was no more.

Linda closed her eyes and pressed finger and thumb to her forehead as the consciousness of this beautiful yet deadly silent planet drove deep into her. She was sprawled in the dry, warm grass, the remains of the picnic around her and Holt close by. He watched her action and then knitted his own brows. Tapping Linda on the arm he motioned for her to lip read.

'What's the matter, Lin? More than usual, I mean.'

'Frankly, I'm wondering what's the use of going on living when there's no sound any more! I don't think I'm going to be able to endure it, Holt!'

'Nerves, purely.' He gave a shrug. 'It's getting you down a bit, but you'll bob up again after a while. All a matter of getting used to it. Everybody has to do that — as most folk are. The death and suicide list isn't nearly long as it was at the beginning. The human animal can get used to anything, Lin. Even this — and whatever else there may be.'

Linda gave a sharp look. 'You haven't

special knowledge of anything even more disastrous yet to come, have you?'

'No — but I wouldn't put anything past D-D. The only way to look at this business is to assume that you've become totally deaf, and let it go at that. Hundreds of thousands who have thus become afflicted don't wail about it. They face it courageously.'

'That's somehow different.' Linda looked about her on the muted fields. 'Very different. That's a personal affliction that you know you can't escape. This is worldwide and terrifying because of it. Look at the disorganization, the misery, the social unrest, the tragedies. You can regard it detachedly because you're a scientist, I suppose, and always more or less preoccupied. But I can't.'

'Then what do you suggest?'

'I'm still wondering, in spite of your statement to the press, whether there isn't some way out — by going to another world.'

He smiled wryly and shook his head. 'Forget it, Lin. In a few months every planet in the system will be as quiet as

41

this one — quite apart from the fact that all of the planets are totally uninhabitable with either poisonous atmospheres or almost no atmosphere at all — '

'But why limit things to this Solar System of ours? Aren't there other systems? Other planets?'

'There most certainly are, but even if there are any capable of supporting our type of life we'd die of old age long before we could possibly reach them! No, Lin, there's no immediate answer to this one, but — but,' he finished slowly, as the girl watched his mouth intently, 'there may be a long term one.'

'What?' Eagerness leapt into her eyes. She had such infinite faith in her husband that she knew if he said a thing could be done there was no doubt whatever about it.

'Too early to say now. I've got to know a lot more about the D.D. before I attempt anything — even a theory. But I'm scientist enough to believe that there's an answer to every physical law, or infraction thereof, and I shall never rest until I find it.'

'Something to lift the Silence, you mean?'

'Much more than that. Something to destroy the D.D. altogether. But it's all a question of time.'

Linda's lips did not move again for a long interval. Holt lay sprawled, his eyes fixed absently on drifting cumulus to the south. It was obvious his keen, scientific mind was infinitely preoccupied; then, as Linda touched his arm, he looked at her again.

'I was reading yesterday about some newly-born children, Holt. The specialists said their ears and auditory nerves were not even developed. What's your opinion of that? Sounds horrifying to me. Even if the Silence lifts the children will never be able to hear.'

Holt brooded through a long interval, then: 'The explanation of that is mainly pre-natal, caused by the shock to mothers at finding all sound at an end. It has been reflected in the children and produced offspring that have no *need* to hear. It is either that or else Nature, in her inscrutable way, is beginning to produce a new form of human being that will have no need of auditory nerves in future. Therein lies real cause for alarm, Lin, because Nature is infinitely cleverer than us — may know that sound is never going to come back and is making the necessary economy in human structure already.'

'Science! Science!' Linda threw up her hands in a deprecating gesture. 'Can't you ever think as a man, Holt, and not as a scientist? What's going to be our reaction if *our* baby is born like that, too?'

'Our baby?' He looked vaguely astonished, and then suddenly eager. 'Great heavens, you don't mean — '

'Yes.' Linda nodded quietly. 'Dr. Bradbury told me about it yesterday. Remember, I went to him for a check up? He or she will be born early next year — into *this*!' Linda's mouth tightened in sudden viciousness. 'Maybe that's why I feel this nightmare more than you do. Where's the *sense* of bringing a child, and probably one without hearing, into a world like this? It would be better dead — and so would I!'

'Oh, come now!' Holt stirred from his

lounging position and threw an arm about the girl's shoulders. 'A great deal can have happened by early next year. The 'radisound' apparatus will be well on the way by then, and speech may be possible if nothing else.'

'Which means you expect our baby to wander through life with a pair of head-phones, or something, strapped round his head?'

'Better than being entirely deaf, isn't it?' Holt was beginning to look irritated, quite incapable of viewing the matter from a potential mother's standpoint.

'I — I don't know what to think.' There were tears in Linda's eyes. 'And just how do you mean? Speech will be possible, *if nothing else*. Won't the 'radisound' make all things bearable again?'

Holt relaxed again and shook his head. 'Afraid not, Lin. The sounds of other things are just not there in the first place, so no apparatus can bring them to audibility. Speech is a different thing entirely. I'm hoping it may be transmitted and received electrically. If that can be done the various governments of the world will provide apparatus for every living soul who, in the normal way, is capable of hearing.'

'Including infants and children?'

'Definitely. They're even more important than the adults if it comes to that — all their lives before them.'

'A nation of telephonists!' Linda sighed to herself. 'That is what they'll look like! And supposing the 'radisound' fails to work?'

Holt shrugged. 'Have to think of something else. And that will take time.'

Linda 'said' no more and Holt wondered anxiously what kind of thoughts were chasing through her mind. He did not question her, however; he knew too well his own faults and was afraid that his apparently callous outlook on things would disturb the girl still more. As things were she was better left alone. But Holt made a vow to himself: that the 'radisound' equipment *must* be made to work, no matter what the cost or the endeavour.

The moment his vacation was over, and the Silence remained undisturbed, Holt threw himself with a new zest into the problems of the 'radisound', discovering that Luther had made quite fair progress on the electrical side of the apparatus, but had not yet perfected the transmission of perfect audible speech.

For two more weeks, backed by all the resources of the laboratory, and calling in the best brains in sonics and sound transmission for their specialised knowledge, Holt and Luther laboured with the equipment, until at the end of this time they had it as near perfect as they could hope to get it. The time had come for the test.

Holt chose to be at the receiving end — seated at the furthest corner of the laboratory — and Luther handled the transmission. The equipment consisted of a tight rubber mask which — in the fashion of the one-time Frogmen — fitted tautly over the nose and mouth, thereby completely trapping the air which lay within the mask and which was supplied from a small cylinder fitted on the back of the wearer. In this way the sounds emitted by the voice were unable to escape from the region of the mask and were instead transmitted into a highly sensitive microphone on the mask front. Indeed, the microphone was also a radio set of exquisite miniature design and ought to transmit the voice over a range of perhaps twelve feet.

Complementary to the transmitting microphone were the earphones, fitting with uncomfortable tautness over the ears, to exclude all air escape, and wired to the tiny radio equipment. A simple switch changed the apparatus from transmission to reception, making it possible — it was hoped — to speak or listen at will. Definitely the whole apparatus was clumsy and decidedly uncomfortable, but if the principle was correct the modifications could soon follow. The next few minutes would decide.

So Holt sat at one end of the laboratory and Luther at the other, the various scientists who had worked on the apparatus standing around watching intently. Finally Holt raised his hand to signal that he was ready for reception. The strained look on his craggy face was sufficient evidence of how much this test meant to him — and indeed to everybody in the muted world.

Luther nodded and Holt waited. He went on waiting, second after second, until half a minute had gone by. The scientists glanced at one another anxiously; then at last Luther got quickly to his feet and came across the laboratory, scribbling a note as he moved. Holt took it and read:

'Didn't you hear me? I identified myself and asked several questions.'

With a sinking heart Holt scribbled his answer: 'Not a sound. The earphones were as dead, and still are, as though disconnected.'

The two men looked at each other dumbly for a moment, then Luther signalled and they began a careful check-up of the apparatus, making sure that every wire and terminal was in its right place. The more they investigated the more their spirits sank. No mistakes had been made. Everything was just as it should be — and yet voice transmission was not possible. So they tried other sounds, placing the objects in sealed chambers and wiring them up, but in every case the answer was the same. The wall of silence was not breached.

An hour had gone by before Luther attempted to answer the riddle. Holt and the scientists gathered around him as he scribbled on the notepad.

'The only solution, gentlemen, is that the dyno-depressant, in its present activity at least, is affecting the electrical particles inherent in every sound wave. That includes the small content of air behind the masks we have devised. To transmit any sound demands air, of course, but even air cannot do it if the particles themselves are blanked out by an electrical force that prevents their normal action. My considered opinion is that any effort to create sound under the present circumstances must be abandoned.'

This was a statement that had the knell of doom about it. Holt clenched his fists and looked at Luther sharply, to be met with a negative shake of the head. Luther meant exactly what he said, and as one of the greatest living sonic experts his opinion had to be respected.

Holt whipped out his own notepad and wrote swiftly, handing it to Luther:

'Since we've failed in our effort we are compelled to advise the clamouring public of the fact — but we just can't give them a plain tale of disaster and offer them nothing to cling to. I suggest we attempt an expedition into space — with the cooperation of the European Space Agency — and see if we can judge when the D-D is likely to stop exerting its influence. There is an end to everything. Surely there must be a foreseeable end to this?'

Luther mused over the note for a while and then finally gave a nod of assent. The remaining scientists also read the message and were quick in their acquiescence. Any kind of action was better than sitting around absorbing the crushing load of defeat.

So these new plans were put in hand, governments were informed, and the European Space Agency contacted and ordered to prepare a spaceship for the mission. The deaf-mute public was told through newspapers that science was doing its utmost to get things in hand.

Since this tale had been told at varying intervals ever since the Silence had clamped down, nobody believed it any more. Most realised by now that science was licked but unwilling to admit the fact.

And the debit and credit side of the disaster continued to expand. On the debit side were the untold thousands who had been thrown out of work and who seemed unlikely to get any unless the Silence lifted. They either starved — there just was not enough benefit to go round — or else turned to crime, taking advantage of the eternal quietness to rob and pillage as they chose. Consequently the law had a twenty-four hour job on its hands trying to keep the peace.

Those who were fortunate enough to still be working, and to whom the Silence represented little more than a considerable inconvenience, were quite philosophic and even good-humoured about the business, and it was because they represented the bulk of the community that matters did not get entirely out of hand. For, after all, business could still proceed even without sound. The trade of the world continued after its initial interruption, and slowly but surely, men and women in every clime were learning the universal sign language. In one way the Silence was producing that unification for which the more high-minded diplomats had struggled for years without success.

Some men and women even pointed out the advantages of Silence. Their examples were trivial, yet true. The neighbour's children could no longer be a nuisance, especially with a piano; there was no trouble any more from over-loud radio sets bawling at those who were not even remotely interested. Into the discard had gone the nerve-shattering 'inventions of the devil' such as pneumatic drills, improperly silenced motor cycles, jet planes, the thunder of trains over iron bridges, and even the homely vacuum cleaner. True, all these objects were still used, but with the mute hand upon them. There were reports, also, that factory workers whose nerves had been tried to breaking point by the incessant din, were in far better health than before, working amidst thundering machinery and never hearing the slightest whisper.

Amusements had ceased except in visual form. Old-style music hall acts that did not rely on sound were revived and became popular on television. Mime had also come into its own, played without music. Talking films and radio had completely ceased. Perhaps the most popular entertainment of all, apart from muted television, was the silent picture house. Here, in a vast chain of cinemas, Samuel T. Glotzenhimer was reaping a rich harvest.

On the millionaire list now stood the paper manufacturers, the producers of pens, inks, and pencils; the computer and mobile phone manufacturers, and the organisers of the universal sign-language system and publishers. Into Limbo had gone the radio and television kings and queens, the singers, the musicians, the composers, the actors and actresses — save for the percentage who had drifted into 'silents' — the sound engineers, the tele-phonists, radio-operators . . . and so on, down the endless list. The upheaval was colossal and it was only by degrees that

Mankind had the chance to appreciate how much sound is essential to the daily curriculum.

The unchanged ones seemed to be the scientists, Holt Rankin amongst them. Though he personally did not refer to the failure of the 'radisound' equipment he knew that Linda must know all about it since it had been freely publicised in the newspapers. He wondered vaguely why she made no reference to it — until one morning whilst he was at the laboratory he received a messenger from the general hospital.

Surprised, he took the note handed to him. It was signed by the hospital supervisor and said:

★ ★ ★

'You are requested to be present immediately at the above hospital (Ward 3) where your wife, Linda, is dangerously ill following a fall downstairs.'

★ ★ ★

Holt asked silent questions of the messenger, mutely cursed the everlasting Silence, and then wrote a note quick on his pad:

'What are the facts? What happened to make my wife fall downstairs?'

From the shrug in response it appeared that the messenger did not know the answer. So Holt dropped everything immediately and reached the hospital ten minutes later. He was permitted five minutes with the white-faced, scarcely breathing Linda. She was barely conscious, and certainly in no condition to write the words which her lips were trying inadequately to frame — so inadequately indeed that he could not read them. All he could do was stare dumbly, hold her hand, and then leave her. He sought out the doctor in charge of the case and whipped his notebook out of his pocket. The medico shook his head and instead used the universal sign language.

'I thought it advisable to send for you, Mr. Rankin, in view of your wife's low condition.'

'What happened exactly? She was all

right when I left home this morning. Moody, perhaps, but physically well enough.'

'All I know is that a neighbour called at your home — a Mrs. Tadworth, whom you probably know — to borrow something. It would appear that your wife leaves the lounge French windows open for the trades people, there being no other way for them to make themselves heard. This neighbour entered by that means and found your wife lying at the foot of the stairs. She texted for an ambulance and wrote out for us the statement I've just given you.'

Holt frowned, then signalled: 'But why on earth should falling downstairs put my wife in so dangerous a condition? What did she do? Break her spine, or something?'

'Internal injury, Mr. Rankin. I assume you are aware that your wife would have had a child in a few months?'

'So she told me, but — '

'She will not have one now. The damage she brought on herself has precluded that possibility. We're doing all we can to save her, naturally, but you must stand by. You can be reached at the laboratory? Your neighbour seemed to think you could be — '

'Yes, yes, I'll stay there. Keep me posted.'

Dazed, Holt took his departure, and for the rest of the day he was worse than useless at his laboratory work. His fellow scientists, knowing a good deal was amiss because of the hospital call, were not too exacting. Luther, however, who had no time for anything but science and who regarded domestic entanglements as sheer foolery, was anything but tolerant. And towards six that evening his sign language showed it.

'Am I working on these details for the space-laboratory by myself, Rankin, or are you still with me?'

Holt jerked himself out of moody preoccupation and looked at the drafting board. Upon it was the result of many hours of work by the scientists in general and Luther in particular — the design of a testing laboratory to be carried aboard a spaceship, fitted as far as possible with the instruments necessary to analyse the baffling dyno-depressant field.

Luther raised his eyebrows to implement his question, as Holt forced himself to a response.

'I am still with you, Luther. Forgive my absent-mindedness. I'm expecting to hear every minute that my wife is dead.'

'So I understand from the others — but this is not a time for individual troubles. We are working for the good of everybody, or at least we hope so, and I must have your attention.'

Holt felt for a moment that he would very much have liked to hit Luther on the jaw; then he checked himself. After all, the man was right. He had only the chief of the laboratory with whom he could converse, so it was up to Holt to fulfil his obligations.

'In case you haven't completely followed matters,' Luther's signalling resumed, 'this is the sketch for a space laboratory. I don't think you'll find much the matter with it, but if you do let me know. Otherwise it can be put into construction tomorrow. The sooner we get out into space and make what analysis we can the better.'

'I'll study it all night,' Holt promised. 'I shall not be going home. I'm nearer the hospital here should I be wanted.'

Luther nodded and took his departure. One by one the staff also went, leaving Holt gazing at the design under the strong overhead lamps. But he was not seeing the lines, figures, angles and formations. He was picturing Linda's white face and her soundlessly moving lips.

Fallen downstairs? Fallen! Why should she? She was young, not given to vertigo, and the carpet was in perfect order. Had it been a fall, or had it been deliberate? Was the root cause of the trouble the failure of the 'radisound'? Rather than bring a child into a silent world had she deliberately let it be destroyed?

Holt's jaw tightened over this thought. The one thing he wanted outside of Linda and science was a son or daughter. If she had prevented him from having either, perhaps for good, he didn't particularly care what happened to her. No, that was not true. He did care. She was all he had, and if she died he just didn't give a damn whether the Silence ever lifted or not. Even less would he care about trying to overcome it. Without incentive he might just as well be dead, too.

He started as he realised the night watchman was at his side. Silently, with his gap-toothed grin, the old man put down a plate of sandwiches and a flask of tea, then shuffled on his way. Holt gave him a brief smile of thanks and moodily consumed the refreshments as he tried again to pin himself down to studying the plans of the space-laboratory.

Yes, it seemed all right. Good enough. Luther would not make mistakes — Be hanged to it! What about Linda?

To his surprise, towards eight-thirty, Luther returned. He moved with his usual businesslike air, heading across the expanse and asking a question on his fingers as he approached:

'Been through it yet? I've been seeing the responsible men in the government and they've asked me to hurry things up. The only thing that will placate the public is a forecast of how long the Silence will last. We've got to find out, if only for the sake of the women.'

Holt started, began with signs: 'Why the women particularly?'

'Because they're causing more trouble than the men. The men can stand the Silence: the women can't. Remember, they are the progenitors of the race, and when they refuse in their tens of thousands to have children, and even contemplate murdering those they have, something has to be done to reassure them. If that isn't done the race will be extinct in a century. I got the statistics from the government whilst I was there. It appears that women everywhere are reacting almost identically to the Silence. They just will not contemplate bringing babies into it — and I don't blame them.'

'Which makes my wife no exception.' Holt's fingers moved restlessly. 'I can't blame her when nearly all women are behaving the same way. As to this — ' He gestured to the drawing-board. 'As to this, I can't see anything wrong with it. Carry on by all means.'

Methodically Luther unpinned the design from the board and rolled it up.

'I'll let the government have it immediately. They'll work with the European Space Agency to have it constructed and installed aboard a specially-modified spaceship. In the meantime we will have to undergo special training to be ready for the rigours of the flight itself. You, of course, will come with us into space?'

'If my wife lives, yes. If there's still doubt I shall stay here.'

Luther looked irritated. 'Must I repeat, this is no time for personal problems?'

'My wife means more to me than any damned dyno-depressant!' Holt's jaw set stubbornly. Then he glanced up quickly as a hospital messenger entered the laboratory and looked about him. Seeing Holt he came quickly forward, removing an envelope from the wallet on his belt.

Holt nearly snatched the missive, ripped the envelope, and read the note within:

★   ★   ★

'*Glad to advise you that crisis in connection with your wife has now passed and there is no reason to suppose but that her recovery will be complete. — J. L. Meadows,*
  Superintendent.'

★ ★ ★

Holt signalled a brief thanks to the messenger and then turned to the waiting Luther. His fingers moved again.

'I'll be coming into space. Everything's all right.'

'I'm glad. And get some rest. You look as though you need it.'

3

Into space

In the days that followed, whilst the space laboratory was being built and the precision instrument makers were hard at it, the European Space Agency were also working flat out to modify a spaceship that could incorporate it, and to prepare a crash training regime for the scientists. Holt moved religiously between the laboratory and the hospital, cheerfully nonetheless since Linda was making rapid strides to recovery. So far he had not questioned her as to her 'accident.' He reserved this until the evening she came home, the day before he was due to leave for Europe to begin his training preparatory to the flight itself.

'If that fall you took was deliberate, then admit it,' Holt insisted, as the girl read his lips. 'I'm not going to hold it against you because most of the women are reacting in the same way,'

'Yes — it was deliberate.' Linda's dark eyes searched Holt's face as she answered. 'I wanted even more to kill the unborn. I wanted to kill myself — and I still want to!'

'But for heaven's sake, why?' Holt seized her shoulders. 'I know the Silence is maddening, but it's no worse for you than for anybody else, and look how everybody else is putting up with it, and smiling.'

'Maybe that's because they don't know what I know.'

Holt frowned. 'Know what? Something you've been hiding?'

'Yes. Has it ever occurred to your scientific mind what happens to something, particularly a human organ, which is never used?'

'Well? It perishes, of course. If you don't use your hand it finally withers. If you don't use your legs they fail you . . .' Holt stopped, his lips half open, then he resumed quickly, 'Linda, what are you telling me?'

'I'm telling you that my ears — and

probably yours and everybody else's are dying internally through not being able to function. Dr. Bradbury told me when he checked up on me that my ears would probably not function again even if sound did come back. Nor is my case isolated. Thousands of men and women, according to him, are all in the same plight. My reaction to that was that I didn't want to live any more. Not in a world of eternal quiet. Maybe your ears are the same way. Why don't you check up?'

Holt shook his head. 'I don't believe it, and Bradbury ought to be more careful with his diagnosis. Neither he nor anybody else can tell whether an ear can function properly without a sound to test it. Forget it, Linda. It's true that an organ that is unused loses its faculty, but that takes a very long time. Years at least. You've been needlessly scared — Different matter about the baby, of course. I can understand that you didn't want it born into a world like this.'

Linda gave a wistful smile. 'Thanks for the reassurance, Holt, but you're not doing it very well. Bradbury knows what he's talking about and it seems to me that for practically everybody in the world it doesn't matter whether the Silence lifts or not. We'll none of us know the difference.'

Which was more than enough for Holt. Ten minutes later he left Linda in charge of the companion nurse he had hired for the occasion and visited Bradbury. The genial old family physician remained unshaken by Holt's fierce denouncements and finally finger-signed his answer.

'You're a good scientist, Mr. Rankin, but it doesn't embrace the medical field, that's obvious. There is such a thing as the pressure of silence, remember. That reacts very unfavourably on the ears, especially if maintained indefinitely. I myself have diagnosed some fifty cases of aural atrophy, and if you enquire further you'll find I'm not alone.'

Holt did enquire further, that very night, mainly from the headquarters of the Health Ministry, and in the end he was forced to the conclusion that a new horror had been added to the Silence. In the vast majority of cases, unless the medical experts had utterly misread the signs, there would be thousands of souls from whom the Silence would never lift.

Just the same, though he bowed to the weight of opinion, Holt was not entirely convinced. As a scientist he still believed that the condition outlined by the medicals as being actually in being could only appear after many years, and he also deprecated the fact that the medicals insisted on headlining their views across the front pages of the next morning's newspapers.

'I'll prove 'em wrong,' he told Linda fiercely, as she read his lip movements at breakfast. 'But for their cockeyed theories you'd never have thrown yourself downstairs as you did — and probably thousands of other women wouldn't be so damned scared as they are now. The space experiments we intend to make will show just how long the Silence is likely to last and what has been happening to you, and your mind, makes me determined to get a result even if we stay in space for years!'

Linda smiled listlessly. 'Bring back some good kind of news, Holt, and maybe we can start our lives over again, too. Bring back bad news and it doesn't matter much how soon I die, or you too.'

Holt's lips did not move. He felt it useless to point out that Linda's consistently pessimistic attitude was no help to him in the struggle he was making to get things to rights. The only thing he did feel grateful for was that her attitude at least gave him an incentive. He knew he had got to find some hopeful answer or else lose her altogether. She was at the stage where she would obviously not be able to absorb an admission of failure.

So in anything but a happy mood he finally set off for the physical laboratories once more. Upon arrival he discovered that a specially charted jet plane had arrived according to schedule and was standing on the proving ground to the rear of the enormous laboratory buildings. Around it men were at work loading in the various sections of the space laboratory and specially devised instruments that would be transferred and reassembled in the mission spaceship.

Holt surveyed the plane from a

distance, then he went into the building and sought out Luther. He found him in the main laboratory, checking over the last details. To his surprise there was a slim-waisted young woman with him, dressed in conventional slacks and a grey silk blouse. She looked around thirty, was fair-haired, and reasonably good looking.

'This is my secretary, Viola Shawn,' Luther introduced, in the sign language. 'Meet Holt Rankin, Viola, the laboratory chief.'

She smiled brightly and shook hands and Holt found himself marvelling that a woman could look so cheerful amidst such depressing conditions, or had he got Linda too much on his mind?

'A pleasure,' Holt signalled back; then turned to Luther.

'I noticed the plane out on the grounds. How are things? I take it that once the space laboratory is loaded, we'll be going with it?'

'We shall be in about an hour,' Luther responded. 'Everything is being arranged as we planned it. Our own luggage has been chosen for us and is already on board. How's your wife?'

'Depressed. Chiefly because of the ear trouble splashed around by the newspapers.'

Viola gave a disbelieving smile. 'The medical experts would do better to stay out of the field of pure science, if you ask me! The dead silence on everything could not cause ears to lose their power so quickly. I just don't believe it. Why, there have been cases of people locked up or buried away from all sounds for years, but their hearing was not impaired when they came to using it again.'

'I'm glad you think that way Miss Shawn.' Holt gave her a grateful glance. 'Every woman, including my wife, seems to think the Silence is the end of the world.'

'Those who are not scientists probably do think that way. Fortunately I have the outlook of a physicist. Since I am one that is perhaps not surprising.'

'You will be coming on the journey?' Holt questioned.

'I'm looking forward to it. Mr. Luther

needs me at his right hand — as always.'

Holt, with depressing memories of the pessimistic Linda, felt immediately that Viola Shawn was a girl worth knowing. She smiled all the time and yet had the outlook of a scientist. That she was also to accompany the men on the trip into space would certainly make the voyage less monotonous than an all male affair.

Holt had quite a few things he would liked to have said to the girl at that moment, only opportunity did not permit. The supervisor in charge of loading up the plane arrived to signal that all was in order, which meant it was time to begin the journey.

'We're coming,' Luther signalled back, and then turned to Holt. 'The Europeans are providing two astronauts who will actually fly the mission. We will be passengers, and free to carry out our scientific tests in our own section of the modified spaceship. I have assumed the responsibility for that, since the space laboratory is primarily my own design. The actual investigation into the dyno-depressant, however, will be your province. You are more conversant with it than I am. Is that agreed?'

Holt nodded promptly, at which Luther seemed satisfied. He led the way across the laboratory, stepping aside to let Viola Shawn go ahead of him as the open doorway was reached — then all three of them crossed the open space to the waiting plane.

'I suppose,' Viola Shawn remarked, her long, immaculate fingers working swiftly as she walked between Luther and Holt, 'that we ought to regard this as a tremendous thrill — our first voyage into space. Yet somehow it doesn't thrill me a bit. Space is so well known from astronomical observation, and the effects we are likely to encounter so entirely predetermined, that there's no novelty in it.'

'You are not even the faintest bit frightened?' Holt asked.

'Frightened! A scientist cannot afford to be frightened. Fear is the precursor of failure.'

Holt smiled to himself, still marvelling that two women could be so apart in outlook as Linda and Viola Shawn. At home, Linda was presumably waiting tautly for some good news, and determined to make a nuisance of herself if she did not get it; yet here was this young woman, her clear blue eyes unafraid, entirely willing to risk the gamble of a flight into outer space with only four men for company. It made Holt wonder why he had not met her years earlier. She was unmarried — her left hand showed it — and Luther plainly regarded her as just an efficient secretary. Anything in the nature of romance was coldly abhorrent to his calculating, scientific mind.

They entered the plane and were shown to their seats. Within minutes they were in the air.

Arriving at the European Space Agency, they were met on leaving the plane by officials and technicians. They also met the two astronauts who would pilot the ship into space, and in whose experienced hands they were in truth entrusting their lives.

Over the next two weeks, Holt's admiration for Viola Shawn increased even more, as she underwent a crash course in space-training, along with the two men. At times it was quite exhausting, as they were whirled around in an apparatus that Holt, as a physicist, thought resembled a cyclotron. This simulated the accelerative pressures they would experience at take-off. Holt's admiration for Luther, too, increased. Whilst coldly scientific, the older man took the punishing regime without complaint. Less punishing, but just as disconcerting, were their high-altitude flights that — briefly — accustomed them to the effects of free fall, and lack of gravity. They completed their training by getting accustomed to their cumbersome spacesuits, and the layout of their spaceship. There was the main control room, manned by the two pilots: beyond it lay the passage way leading to the sleeping cubicles, provision and storage departments, and — towards the stern — the big transparent space which would be used for observations. In the stern itself were the massive rocket engines.

Finally the day of the take-off arrived, and all final checks were completed by technicians as the crew, space-suited, were strapped into their pressure bunks. Normal radio contact between Control and the pilots was of course impossible, and instead they had to rely on small individual vision screens on which text messages were displayed, and to which they were able to responded on a small keypad.

The countdown concluded itself, and at zero the lift-off commenced amidst a tremendous explosion of incandescent gases from the stern rocket jets.

The space machine instantly took to the air with the grace and speed of an eagle. Then came the inertia load, dragging down as it seemed with the force of countless tons. Holt and Viola Shawn breathed heavily, fighting to retain their senses. Luther glanced at them, his face wet with perspiration, but not for an instant did the ship's two pilots attempt to relax the acceleration. To do that would cause the vessel to lose its initial momentum and it would drop back to Earth.

Even so there was a limit to what the barely-trained human frame could stand.

Luther himself, being the eldest, throwing more strain on his heart, was the first to faint. To Holt the pressures around him felt like solid concrete and he was forced to lie completely immobile. He managed a glance across at Viola Shawn and saw that she too had succumbed. Then his own senses left him. Controlled with consummate skill by the two experienced astronauts who remained fully conscious throughout, the ship flew onwards with mounting velocity until it reached the prescribed maximum, Here the rockets ceased firing and all acceleration, and therefore inertia, stopped.

With all the pressure relaxed Holt recovered and found himself completely weightless. As he had been trained to do, he 'floated' himself out of his bunk and to the observation window, absorbing the wonder of the view. Earth lay to the apparent rear — 20,000 miles away according to the instruments — and in every other direction lay the diamond-bright hosts of heaven. For just a moment Holt was puzzled by the fact that not all of the Milky Way Galaxy seemed to be in view — only part of it, but he had no time then to consider this fact.

Turning, he moved towards Viola Shawn and helped her to 'drift' from the pressure rack. She said something quickly, with a vaguely nervous smile, then recalling the ever-present Silence, which was evidently operative here in space as well, she used the usual sign language.

'This weightlessness is amazing! Just like sitting on balloons!'

Holt nodded and grinned, then turned to Luther and helped him back to consciousness. Each one of them took a small dose of brandy squeezed from a tube, and then made their way to the transparent observation chamber at the rear of the ship, leaving the two pilots at the control panels. They merely smiled and exchanged the 'thumbs up' sign.

It took courage to enter the observation chamber. The absolute total black of space and the lack of bright light in the chamber, which prevented any reflections, made it appear that they were stepping from the metal passageway into sheer space, the transparent floor being invisible. Luther was the only one who literally took it in his stride, concentrated as usual on the scientific issues — but for a while Holt and the girl stood looking down between their feet at the endless depth of infinity and the oceans of stars which swam therein. It was a giddying, nerve-racking sensation and presently produced such a conviction of headlong falling that they had to look up and around them to steady themselves.

Even through the walls and roof the view was identical except where the bulk of the instruments or telescope made an obstruction. Then Luther switched on subsidiary light and the surroundings assumed a more normal aspect.

'We did not come into space for the purpose of sight-seeing,' his hands said. 'Impressive though the view is. We must take advantage of having the nose of the ship to the sun, which prevents his brilliance interfering with our observations. If you are ready?'

Feeling thoroughly chastened Holt and the girl both nodded, Holt moving to the instrument panels and the girl opening her notebook to take down whatever information Luther signalled to her.

The moment he found himself with the instruments to deal with Holt was the scientist again. He forgot all about the side issues and the delectable Viola: he gave his attention to the newly devised instrument for measuring the intensity and range of the dyno-depressant field. Nor was it particularly cheering to find the instrument registering a maximum load.

'At least we have found equipment which reacts to this new type of electricity,' was Holt's signalled observation. 'So far we have had no proper reaction through not knowing what we were dealing with.'

Luther nodded briefly, his keen eyes on the gauges. There was no doubt in his mind, or Holt's either, trained as they were to reading the scientific signs, that the dyno-depressant field was almost infinite in extent.

'Perhaps,' Viola signalled, also looking at the instruments since she had no notes to take at the moment, 'we happen to be in the exact centre of the field, or thereabouts, which will, of course, give us the greatest reading distance?'

Luther gave a nod of admission, then: 'I think we might do better if we travelled outwards, away from the Earth, following the course this D-D field took as it approached. It came originally from the region of the First Galaxy, the Milky Way. If, several millions of miles further away from Earth than we are now we find a weakening of the load, we'll know that there is a chance of it finally passing by.'

The decision taken they acted upon it, Luther texting a message to the pilots on his portable handset as they made their way back to the control room.

So, at a speed which was leisurely as space distances go, but incredibly fast when measured beside any Earth journey, they swept outwards into space, heading beyond the orbit of the Moon and willing to go far beyond that if need be — indeed as far as their fuel could safely carry them and give them the chance to get back home.

Most of the time the scientists spent

checking their notes and making fresh readings of the D-D field. Holt found a good deal of useful information concerning the 'bastard electricity', but even he was not clever enough to fathom what exactly the energy was. Not that this could be considered surprising since few scientists could properly explain normal electricity, let alone a form of it never before encountered.

The fact remained that as the endless millions of miles were covered there was no alteration in the load-reading. It remained constant which seemed to show it was exerting its influence throughout space — or at least in this particular region of it.

'How did it ever happen in the first place?' This was the question that the exasperated Luther asked time after time with his hand-signals. 'There has to be a cause for everything, Holt, and we're not finding it!'

'Any more than we have ever found the source of cosmic rays,' Holt answered. 'Consider the various unconvincing solutions we have formed to explain them

— the break-up of distant stars releasing their energy; atomic processes going on in the depths of outer space — We really don't know what brought the D-D about. If it should prove that there is no lessening of the field, no matter how far we travel towards its apparent source, it can only mean that maybe space itself has reached a mutation and that the D-D has come to stay.'

Luther gave a sharp glance. 'Mutation? Are you suggesting that even space might mutate?'

'Why not? Everything else does — even metals. In the course of evolution everything changes gradually, and in the process of advancement there are points reached where an absolute change takes place — otherwise known as mutation. Because space has never produced a mutation within recorded knowledge is no reason why it shouldn't do it now.'

'If space mutates, everything else will have to conform to that change.'

'That can and will happen if need be. You can't stop Nature adjusting herself. Change of environment, and the failure of the essential basis of food for them, wiped out the early monsters of the prehistoric Age. There was an example of a mutational change in Earth's structure forcing apparently unchanging species of animals to disappear. If this is a spatial mutation the consequences will be far-reaching — and probably catastrophic as far as we are concerned.'

Holt stopped his restless hand and turned again to the instruments. Then he studied his notes. By degrees he was beginning to sift out the nature of this extraordinary form of electricity, and the more he did so the more there came into prominence in the back of his mind an idea he had always speculated upon to destroy the D-D altogether. It all depended. He had so much more to learn yet. Even if the D-D did represent a mutation it did not make it incapable of destruction. If it could be annihilated it would be a triumph of man's intelligence over the blind forces of the cosmos.

So the vessel still flew onwards, leaving the orbit of the Moon behind and launching out into the greater deeps.

There was fuel enough and to spare — and even had the mission not been so urgent there was the fascination of being drawn further and further towards those remoter worlds, which, up to now, had only been pinpoints in a telescope.

There were of course periods of relaxation, periods when, since the two astronauts were controlling the ship, all three travellers were able to drop their scientific investigation for a while and view the void as sightseers, without trying to analyse it. Holt took advantage of these times to be near Viola. His interest in her had no way waned and her consistently scientific outlook and cheerfulness were both qualities he intensely admired. Not for a moment did he realise that his reactions were entirely normal. Unconsciously he had been shocked by the revelation of Linda's intense selfishness and lack of scientific understanding. The devotion that he had imagined existed had evidently only been of the 'fair weather' variety.

'Supposing,' Holt 'said', as he and Viola sat viewing the deeps of space whilst

Luther browsed through his notes, 'that the Silence never lifts from Earth? That we cannot find an end to the D-D and therefore a cessation of our trouble? What would your reaction be?'

'Grin and bear it, I suppose.' The girl's shoulders moved negatively as her slender hands worked. 'It takes a lot of getting used to, the dead and utter silence and the lack of all familiar sounds which make up the pattern of life — but an intelligent creature should be able to adapt itself to anything and that's what I hope I shall be able to do.'

'You wouldn't commit suicide?'

'Why should I? That's the coward's way out.' Holt was satisfied. Here was a woman as diametrically opposed to Linda as any woman could be. He found himself wondering vaguely what kind of a voice she had — whether it matched the smoothness of her figure and frank cheerfulness of her features. He hoped so. Hard voices jarred on his meditative mind. That was one thing about Linda: she had a gentle voice with no affectation, one of the things that had drawn him to her in the first place.

Holt was pondering over what observation to make next when his gaze, directed through the transparent wall of the observation chamber, settled on the mighty First Galaxy — the Milky Way, and he noticed again that peculiarity about it which he had remarked at the outset of the journey. It definitely looked as though part of it, at the top right hand limb, was out of sight, masked, or somehow rendered invisible. He knew just how the First Galaxy ought to look but for some reason it didn't. Not that he was getting a closer view of the First Galaxy, despite the millions of miles the space machine had covered, for the Milky Way was so far away that whole light-centuries would have to be hurdled before it could be brought any appreciably nearer to the human vision.

Viola's arm nudged and her fingers asked: 'Something the matter? Doesn't the cosmos measure up to your expectations?'

'The Milky Way certainly doesn't. Something queer about it. Take a look.'

Viola gazed at it long and earnestly, for quite three minutes, and at length Holt saw a frown notching her eyebrows. At last her hands moved.

'Part of it is missing — and beyond it there are no stars. It's like a hole in space, if there can be such a thing.'

'Exactly. No stars beyond it. Something resembling the Black Hole in Cygnus. The point is, it ought not to be there!'

Holt glanced across at Luther, busy with his notes, and waited to catch his eye. Then he signalled him. He came across and, the position explained to him by Holt, surveyed the Milky Way pensively. Finally he turned to the telescope and spent five long minutes peering into the deeps. When he looked up again his face was wondering, troubled.

'What?' Holt questioned, his own expression anxious.

'That black segment, whatever it is, is advancing. I could see it happening. Stars are being swallowed up in the process, or if not that, their light ceases to shine.'

His statement was enough to get both Holt and the girl quickly from the window seat. Each in turn they studied the phenomenon through the telescope, and there was no doubt that Luther had been correct. Like slowly spreading black ink darkness was crawling over the face of the Milky Way at the top right hand limb, and though the process seemed slow — no swifter than the rise of a thread of mercury in a warm hand — it must actually have been incredibly fast because of the Milky Way's colossal dimensions.

'What in hell is it?' Holt signalled quickly, baffled.

Luther thought for a moment, then, 'Unless I'm mistaken that is another formation, or development of the dyno-depressant. Perhaps the very core of it, sweeping inwards from its unknown source in the greater deeps beyond the First Galaxy.'

'Then we are actually seeing it now?' Viola asked. 'If you can say that about an advancing stream of darkness.'

Luther shook his head. 'Not that. What is happening, I think, is that the electrical field is now affecting light-waves, far out in space there. Nothing is actually being annihilated. Those stars are not being snuffed out or destroyed: their light is simply ceasing to reach us.'

It was several moments before the full horror of what this implied struck home to Holt. His hands moved again and he cursed the absence of sound in his desire to make so many statements and ask so many questions.

'If this inwardly spreading light-failure reaches us, we're finished. We're handicapped enough as it is. If it goes dark as well we — ' Luther motioned to a flat surface and there he drew a sheet of paper and wrote swiftly, an easier way than constantly using the irritating hand signs. When he had finished Holt and Viola both read:

'My theory is that the Dyno-Depressant is in the form of a circle, in the fashion of waves radiated by dropping a stone into a smooth pond. Such is the character of electrical, radiative action. The source of the actual D-D presumably in the depths of space, from which have flowed the outwardly expanding waves. The outermost have reached the Solar System and their effect has been to neutralise the electrical waves responsible for sound. Now we have deeper influences from the same source that have a different effect, apparently that of cancelling out light-waves on a similar basis — heat, radio waves, ultra-violet, infra-red, and all those in the spectrum, will be cancelled out by this invading field. It is obvious now that we can make no calculation as to the extent of the D-D field. As you know, the instruments still remain at the maximum recording. Far from returning to Earth with a talc of hope I fear we can only bring one of dread — a warning that the failure of light is likely to come soon. This blackout is spreading with appalling rapidity and the sooner we return to Earth the better.'

Once he had read the message through Holt sat with his lips tight for awhile, overwhelmed by a feeling of complete helplessness. He had forseen the possibility of the D-D producing further unwanted effects on the known radiation and electrical waves of material formations, but he had not thought of the failure of light-waves as a possibility.

'This,' said Viola's hands, 'will mean that Mankind, as well as being stone deaf will also be blind, and cold, and lost. It's another way of saying it's the end of the world!'

'Depending,' Luther answered, 'on the extent of this new form of unpleasantness. When the constantly moving waves from the source of this disturbance have passed by us we may start on the 'other side' of the trouble, so to speak. Light may return, then sound: we can't chart it. Its extent may fill all the Universe in which case it may force all the laws which we have considered to be immutable to bend to its new order. It is alien, deadly, and we're utterly at its mercy. To travel any further into the deeps is a waste of time. I'll text the captain to turn the vessel around and head back to Earth.'

4

Rankin's Belt

On Luther's instructions, the captain gave the space machine the maximum of speed and the minimum of comfort in the return journey back to Earth. It was not that he feared the distant darkness would overtake — for it was still a vast distance away — but that he felt the urgent necessity of warning the world of what was to come. Various schemes were chasing through his mind as possible ideas to overcome the prospect of this added horror, but none of them appeared too acceptable.

Holt and Viola Shawn likewise spent much of their time on the return trip discussing by hand signs the new position that had arisen, but this time both of them were faced with a desperate problem. It had been tough enough to partly overcome the handicap of the failure of sound. To overcome darkness and lack of heat as well would be well nigh impossible. The only chance, and a very slim one, was that the onrushing extinction of light-waves might somehow pass the Solar System by. On the other hand, why should it, when the earlier part of the D-D's outflowing waves had completely enveloped the planets of the entire Solar System?

Holt's last message to Viola after reaching Earth and undergoing a medical check — which was positive — was that he would keep in touch with her. This he meant to do at all costs; she was the only feminine element which he considered worth cultivating and he had gathered enough to know that, despite the precarious conditions under which they were living, she also felt attracted to him.

Then, this personal issue decided for the moment, he went with Luther to report the grim news to the Government, with the result that steps were immediately taken to ask the world's astronomers to check up on the possibilities. In space there had not been the necessary instruments to make an exact analysis, nor had there been a 'firm foundation'. A moving spaceship was no place for making mathematically exact forecasts.

So, in the period whilst the reports were awaited, Holt returned home, prepared for the descent of absolute gloom when he hinted at the possibilities for the future. To his surprise, however, he found that Linda was no longer in bed, that the nurse had been dismissed, and that — oddly enough — she was dressed in a neat grey uniform and shirt blouse. She looked more than well: she was radiant.

'Hello, dearest.' Holt's lips formed the greeting as she came towards him with outstretched hands. She had already been informed of his imminent arrival via e-mail.

She kissed him warmly, putting an arm about his waist. He gave her attire a vague glance of wonder and then settled wearily on the settee.

'Apparently you're better again,' his lips said.

'More than better. I've been given a

certificate of an A-1 life by the Medical Authority. On the strength of it I decided to join the Women's Silent Help Army. Better known as the W.S.H.A. It was formed whilst you were away by Gertrude Bracknell, the social reformer. Doing good work, too.'

'And what does this army do?' Holt asked in wonder, as the girl fled towards the kitchen regions to fix him a meal; but since her back was to him she did not get the question and he had to repeat it when she returned with tea and hastily made sandwiches.

'Do?' her mouth repeated. 'Why, we dispense what comfort we can to those who find the Silence overwhelming. We deliver books, free computers and televisions, movie projectors and films, give sign lectures calculated to uplift the depressed spirits, and so on. I think we do a great deal of good.'

'Yes. Yes, I'm sure — ' Holt took a sandwich and munched it absently, struggling to understand what had happened. This was not the Linda he had left: she was a totally different woman.

'But it's you who matters,' she hurried on, sitting beside him and searching his face eagerly. 'What happened in space? Did the trip measure up to expectations?'

'Oh, the trip itself was perfect. We got well out into the depths of space before we returned home.'

'How marvellous! And what about this wretched Silence? When is it going to lift?'

Holt drank some tea before answering. 'Hard to say, Lin. All our analyses aren't completed yet.'

He should have known better than try and deceive her. They had been too long together for her not to interpret every shade of expression.

'That isn't the whole story, Holt,' she stated.

'Well — no, only I don't want to make you miserable again when I've come back to find you so — so improved.'

'You can tell me. My nerves are strong enough again to stand shocks.'

'All right then. You'll know soon enough, anyhow. There is no foreseeable date when the Silence will lift, and the chances are that things may become a good deal worse.'

'Could they? Linda gave a twisted smile.

Holt hesitated, fiddling about with a sandwich he did not really want. His nerves were too strained for him to think about eating.

'There is a possibility, upon which astronomers the world over are now checking, that darkness may be added to the Silence.'

Linda sat staring at him, neither afraid nor moved in any way. It was obvious she had not fully comprehended.

'How?' she asked abruptly. 'You mean the Earth will stop revolving or something, so the sun won't shine on us?'

'I mean darkness in its most absolute sense, Lin. A darkness wherein no light of any kind will function because the dyno-depressant will be so scrambling the lightwaves — as it already has the particles of sound-waves — they won't operate. Out in space we could see the stars winking out in the Milky Way as it approaches. Whether it will involve us,

99

and how soon, is what the astronomers are now trying to discover.'

Linda spread her hands and smiled helplessly. 'But how do we survive such a thing? We only keep going as it is by means of a desperate struggle, lip reading, sign language, and texting and the internet and so on. With light gone and those methods wiped out we'll be finished.'

Holt was silent, waiting for the deluge of gloom. But it did not come.

'I suppose,' Linda 'said' at length, 'a lot will depend on how long such a condition prevails. Possibly we could endure it for a short time — improvise somehow, but if it went on too long we'd just die out.'

'I'm afraid so. Of even greater serious-ness than the possible darkness — though that's bad enough in all conscience! — is the likelihood of heat also failing. In fact it will be bound to do so if light goes because it is in the same order of vibration.'

'How soon will you know?'

'I'm going back to the government headquarters in a couple of hours to get the reports — ' Holt put a hand on Linda's as it lay beside him. 'I must say I'm surprised, and glad, to find you taking the blow so well. I expected something pretty close to hysterics.'

Linda shook her dark head. 'Not this time, Holt. Y'know, when I was left alone after your departure for the space trip I got to thinking, and I'd plenty of time in which to do it. I began to see that as your wife I hadn't measured up to very much. I'd taken all, and given nothing. Even destroyed the one thing you wanted — a child. In my own defence I may say I did that because I believed, and still do, that no child should be born in these conditions, but I also saw how selfish I had become. I tried to look at it from your angle and see the effort you were making, scientifically, to right things. From that moment onwards I decided I ought to be more useful to the community in general and you in particular.'

Holt made no comment: he was still too much astonished. It also made hay of the plans he had formulated in respect to Viola Shawn.

'Tell me more about space,' Linda urged. 'What's it really like?'

Glad of the opportunity to change the subject Holt went into detail concerning his experiences, and inevitably the name of Viola Shawn came into it, but he took good care to only mention it with apparent casualness.

'She must be a woman of unusual accomplishments,' Linda commented.

'Definitely she is. Scientific, good-looking, young, and with more than her share of courage. I confess I felt quite attracted to her.'

'Couldn't be,' Linda responded, shaking her head. 'As a scientist you ought to know that only *opposites* attract, and as far as I can see you and she have identical outlooks.'

'Opposites attract — ' There was a far-away look suddenly in Holt's eyes. 'Like charges repel. The first law of electricity — ' His eyes wandered back to Linda. 'I'm surprised you remember that law.'

'Oh, I did have Grade-A in physics in my schooldays, otherwise I'd never have got that job in the laboratory. About the only thing I do remember though — '

Holt nodded vaguely, obviously following a line of reasoning. In fact Linda's half-joking observation had started a whole sequence of ideas, most of them gradually linking up — or trying to — to that cloudy theory he had to the back of his mind concerning the destruction of the dyno-depressant. When at last he left Linda again to head for the government offices he did so sooner than was necessary, purely to give himself the chance to think without having to answer Linda's quite natural questions.

Once he arrived at headquarters, however, he was forced again to abandon his cogitations before the impact of astronomical discoveries. The expected reports had arrived, sent by e-mail from the far corners of the Earth, and in every degree they coincided. Observation in the Western hemisphere had been prevented by the daylight, but from the East the news was startling — horrifying.

The black gulf was inevitably heading towards the Solar System! Already Hercules, Cygnus, Antares and Vega had disappeared and been replaced by sprawling tentacles of darkness which were stealing across the celestial dome as rapidly as frost fronds on a windowpane. Actually the inwardly spreading dark channels were not moving with great speed — but the Solar System *was*, travelling at a million miles a minute in the general direction of the ever-swelling dark core.

The question now was — how soon? Holt looked up with anxious eyes from the reports and beheld Luther's grim visage. He handed over a final report, a consensus of opinion by all the astronomers.

★　★　★

In our opinion the core of the dyno-depressant, towards which the entire Solar System is moving, as well as the dyno-depressant advancing towards us, will be appreciable to us in approximately 21 days. Since all forms of light and radiation fail to register in the areas that are now blacked out, we can only expect a cessation of the action of light waves, heat waves, and radio waves. From infra red to ultra violet radiation will cease to function. For how long we do not know. This, added to the present total Silence, will undoubtedly be the ultimate Catastrophe, from which we cannot suggest any means of escape.

★ ★ ★

Holt straightened up abruptly, a fierce gleam in his eyes.

'We're not going to sit down to this, are we?' he demanded, using the inevitable sign language. 'We've beaten the Silence and got ourselves passably organised. Life is still going on. We have three weeks in which to think up ways of adapting ourselves to — *this*!'

'Possibly we could find a means of living, even in the Darkness, providing it was not of very long duration,' Luther responded. 'But when this D-D core reaches the sun the last spark of heat will expire as well as light. We'll be on a gradually freezing planet. Then what?'

'Provide everybody with furs,' Holt

replied. 'Outside heat, from radiators, fires, sun, or anything else will cease, yes, but bodily warmth, produced by the change of energy within ourselves, will last as long as we stay alive. Furs will insulate it and keep us warm for some considerable time. That's my suggestion.'

The government experts were nodding slow agreement, but Luther did not appear too impressed.

'It's staving off the evil hour, Rankin, and to what avail? Better to freeze to death and get it over with. I'd agree with you if this D-D core were known to be of comparatively small area, but we can see for ourselves that it extends right across the Milky Way, and far beyond that, without showing any signs of ending. That means it is light centuries in extent and that it will take our Solar System, Earth included, tens of thousands of years to move clear of it. If ever! I incline to your own view that a space mutation has occurred and that the old laws are being destroyed. With the new laws will come a new type of living creature, maybe a mole variety — blind, earless, accustomed to relentless cold, and in time, absence of air — if anything can live. The more I see of this ghastly business the more I realise it is the finish.'

Holt shook his head with sudden fierceness. 'I refuse to subscribe to the view that we're doomed. I agree that the D-D *could* finish us — if we let it. I have an idea which may defeat it, completely dissipate it.'

Luther gave a cold glance of enquiry. He was a highly-trained scientist, a specialist in celestial mechanics in fact, and this statement from the much younger man whose mind cleared to rove inconsequentially between science and romance, was obviously not to his liking.

'You're taking a very wide sweep, Rankin,' he observed at length.

'I know — and I'm not dead sure of myself by any means. I am even less sure that I can develop the idea and put it into practise within three weeks, but if I'm within measuring distance of success at the end of that time we must carry on even if it *is* dark.'

The government leaders glanced at one

another and then at Luther. He was looking at Holt now in frank curiosity. His hands moved swiftly.

'Just what is the basis of the idea? Maybe other views will help you.'

'Doubtless they will, but — ' Holt shifted restlessly, wearied of having to do everything by signs. 'It's all so nebulous in my mind at the moment. I've had the actual idea for a long time, and it has been greatly strengthened by the notes I made in space on the nature of the energy comprising the D-D, but it was a remark of my wife's which started the whole thing revolving in my mind.'

'A remark of your wife's?' Luther's amazement was complete. 'Mr. Rankin, I beg of you to remember that we are fighting a life-and-death issue. I quite fail to see how a remark from your wife can — '

Holt's hands cut him short. 'An apple changed the course of science, didn't it, when Newton watched it fall? Why shouldn't a chance remark do the same?'

'And that is all the information you can give us?' signalled a government expert.

'At the moment it is. I'm going back home to sort out my notes and knock some sense into my idea. When it has reasonable shape I'll explain it to you. I can't do anything in any other direction, anyhow, so I may as well devote myself to my idea. I'll contact you, Dr. Luther, the moment I have something workable.'

Luther nodded as though he never expected such a moment to come to pass, and with that Holt took his departure. In the corridor he collided with Viola Shawn coming in the opposite direction, a bulky file under her arm.

She smiled a greeting and for a moment Holt looked at her vaguely as though wondering who she was. Then he relaxed, returned the smile, and held out his hand.

'Preoccupied, Mr. Rankin?' her sign-language enquired.

'Very. The news about the approaching dark is the very worst, and — '

'I know. I heard earlier. Dr. Luther sent me for the astronomical records so we can figure out more accurately what kind of a path the D-D is taking. It's enough to make any man preoccupied,' the girl finished.

Holt was watching her hands in order to follow her communication, but he forgot the communication in his interest in something else. On the third finger of her left hand there now reposed an engagement and wedding ring. He just could not understand it. He could have sworn they were not there when he had last seen her.

'Did I signal badly?' her hands asked, as he continued to stare at them, and at that he started.

'Sorry. I was just reverting to a personal issue. Have I been incorrect all this time in calling you *Miss* Shawn? I only did so because I didn't observe a wedding ring earlier, and Dr. Luther didn't say whether you were married or not.'

'Yes, I'm married,' her hands answered. 'Very happily too, only I don't use my married name in business. For some reason the high-ups take a dim view of a woman scientist who is also a wife and mother. Actually I'm Viola Heston. Does it matter?'

110

Holt shook his head and made a blundering excuse. 'No — not at all. I made the mistake because of the absence of a ring — '

'I didn't wear it on our space mission because it, and the engagement ring, are made of that new golden-looking metal, *inthanium*. Dr. Luther, being the wise old bird he is, suggested I leave them off in case the free cosmic rays in space made them radio-active. It's that kind of metal — '

'I see.' Holt looked at her steadily and there was mild inquiry in her blue eyes. He realised in that moment that he had come to the very brink of making a complete fool of himself and had just escaped in time.

'Anyway,' his signs continued, 'it was a decided pleasure being with you in space. You may not know it, but the fact that we met as we did may dissolve the D-D. But for my meeting you I wouldn't have mentioned you to my wife, and she wouldn't have made a remark that has given me a great idea. Funny how things work out, isn't it?'

'I suppose it is — when they do.'

Holt smiled a farewell and went on his way, leaving Viola looking rather blankly after him. Like her chief she was wondering if Holt were entirely normal or whether incessant driving work and the deadly load of the Silence were not taking their toll of his mental abilities. They need not have worried. Holt knew exactly what he was doing, so much so that once he had sorted out his notes and started to brood over them he had no awareness of anything else.

Linda, dimly comprehending he had a complex problem to work out, did not disturb him, but she saw to it that he took proper intervals for rest and food.

Meantime the various governments of the world were transmitting the findings of the astronomers to the Press, and they in turn to the general public. The reaction upon a people already depressed and hag-ridden by the everlasting silence was catastrophic for a while. There followed a wave of suicides, murders, settling of old scores, and general end-of-the-world madness, then a more sober spirit prevailed as the majority, rising to new and unexpected heights of courage, set about thinking how best they could overcome this new affliction destined to descend upon them.

In this direction the governments acted on Holt's own suggestion, and the order went forth for the manufacture of fur and arctic clothing in their millions. Everything was thrown into this effort in order that every man, woman and child in the world could be provided for if they desired it: if not, for some personal reason, then they must suffer the consequences. There was no time to discriminate, no time to build special dwellings. Already, in another week, the merciless advance of the core of the D.D was nakedly visible, in that great areas of the sky, at night, were devoid of stars when clouds were not present. The Dark was speeding inwards, the complicated electrical reactions of the dyno-depressant rendering all light-waves void wherever the reacted.

And Holt worked on, sometimes all night and always all day. Whenever Linda went out, either for necessities or to do her share in the W.S.H.A. she always came back to find Holt in his shirtsleeves, blind to time and everything else except the stacks of notes and reference books around him, whilst on bits of paper and in a notepad he had symbols, mathematics, and geometrical designs. He was plainly tired, hollow-cheeked, but still determined.

'Surely,' Linda asked, forcing him to watch her lips as she insisted he take a meal, 'you aren't going to get a solution flogging yourself like this? You're nearly out on your feet.'

'Not yet — and unless I finish what I'm doing *everybody* will be out on their feet, with no chance of recovery. The point is, Lin, that with a bit more work I think I'll have it.'

'Have what?' Linda gently compelled him to start eating. 'You haven't told me anything yet.'

'Only because you're not a scientist, dear. But this much I will say: your comment that opposites attract — implying that like charges repel — certainly started something.'

Linda looked astonished. 'Good heavens, is that what is preoccupying you so much — ?'

'Yes — and I think it's the answer — ' Holt waved a hand. 'But don't disturb me by questions, Lin. I've got the devil of a lot of thinking to do.'

So she let him be. That same afternoon a representative called with the government issue of arctic clothes, at which Holt only glanced and then went on working. From that moment he worked unceasingly until four the following morning, about which time a much worried Linda, fearful for his health under the terrific strains to which he was subjecting himself, crept out of the bedroom to see how he was faring. She had forgotten in her sleepiness that tiptoeing was unnecessary, so hard do ingrained habits die.

He was asleep at the table, head pillowed on his forearm the hand of his other arm still holding the pencil. Linda looked briefly over the notes, failing to make head or tail of them. Carefully she pulled a rug over his shoulders and left him where he was, curling herself up into a nearby armchair so she could keep watch.

In the cold dawn he awoke again, lines under his eyes, a droop to the corners of his mouth, but in spite of all the signs of mental and physical exhaustion Linda could detect the gleam of triumph as he looked across at her.

'I've got it!' his lips said. 'And when I did I fell asleep. For God's sake get me a brandy.'

In a moment Linda had brought it and she spent the next hour until full daylight helping him to collect his notes, setting out his clothes, and seeing to it that he had a good breakfast. She was satisfied, by eight o'clock, that he had weathered the storm into which he had plunged himself. He was dead tired but still alert. The spur seemed to be provided when, over breakfast, he saw the headlines of the morning paper.

FOURTEEN DAYS TO GO!

And underneath these ominous black letters followed a long astronomical account of how far the D-D had crept towards the Solar System, together with corroborative photographs.

'We'll beat it yet!' Holt slapped the paper emphatically. 'I don't guarantee we'll do it in fourteen days but I'm sure we will eventually — Look, Lin, I haven't had the chance to ask you recently, but what are your reactions to all this?'

'More or less negative. You can reach a mental state where after a succession of shocks one more doesn't make any impression. You get sort of punch-drunk. Either way I'm not frightened. I'm all set for whatever turns up.'

Which was enough to satisfy Holt that the metamorphosis from the frightened, pessimistic Linda was complete. In reasonably high spirits he set off after breakfast with his briefcase full of notes, having sent an e-mail ahead of him to Dr. Luther, with a request that he too be present at the government headquarters if at all possible.

As things turned out he arrived only a few minutes after Holt, to find him in consultation with the responsible high-ups.

'Something worthwhile?' Luther's hands signalled briefly. 'I've taken over the job of supervising protective measures for the populace so I can ill afford a single moment away from the task.'

'I'm hoping this will be well worth your while.' Holt quickly pulled forth his notes and designs and spread then on the big table. 'Take a look first and I'll explain it afterwards.'

Luther complied, and so did the government men. As far as the latter were concerned they obviously had not the vaguest idea what was implied. They were concerned with government, not science. Luther, however, was plainly interested — indeed absorbed.

'You gather the drift?' Holt signalled to him.

'Partly. I assume the idea is to fight fire with fire?'

'There's no other way. You can see now why I said a chance remark of my wife's started me off. She said something about 'opposites attract', which immediately put into my mind the fact that like charges repel. I already had all the necessary notes concerning this D-D scourge, its nature, rate of vibration, and so forth.

What I have done is work out how we can produce an electrical field identical to that of the dyno-depressant. The direction of the D-D's influence is *downward*, towards us from outer space. If we release an identical form of energy *upward*, from Earth, we get the necessary parallel of like energies which produces repulsion; this is common law in electrics, and it is more than likely that the two charges, brought into conflict, will cancel each other out and the whole thing — the D-D and our own generated field — will break down and put things right again.'

'A kind of artificial variation of a thunderstorm?' Luther asked. 'I grant you the possibilities, but I reserve my opinion as to what kind of upheaval will occur if the two charges *do* neutralise themselves. The 'recoil', as it were, will travel right out into space with perhaps world-shattering consequences.'

Holt nodded. 'Probably — but that's better than being doomed, isn't it? We certainly will be if we don't act.'

Luther reflected for a while, then: 'Our own field is going to be extremely small compared to the vast field of the D-D.'

'That doesn't signify. Cancel out only part of it and the rest will also collapse. An electrical field is little better than a bubble of vibration. Rupture any part of the field and the entire balance is destroyed and dissipates. I'm convinced the idea will work, but we obviously cannot build the necessary generators and projectors in fourteen days.'

Luther turned quickly to the government experts. They had gathered the drift of the conversation — that there was a chance of beating disaster if Holt's simple yet effective plan worked — but in the matter of manufacturing equipment and having it transported, together with all the demands of labour attaching thereto, they would have to issue the directives.

The head of the high-ups did not demur for a moment. All he asked was for the necessary designs, and everything else would automatically follow. Thus Holt set in motion another tremendous labour drive, as he had with his suggestion of fur coats and protective covering. With two ideas he had become the most important man in the country, perhaps even in the world — and as such he was granted every facility to supervise the plan he had launched.

In the ensuing days he and Luther went everywhere together by fast jet plane, inspecting the gradual development of the generators and projectors in the industrial region not only of England but in the countries abroad that had agreed to adopt the plan. Sites were also selected and each one was calculated to be about 250 miles from its neighbour, all of them forming a girdle about the Earth and called by some newswriters 'Rankin's Belt'.

To these sites armies of men were rushed, each one supplied with protective arctic clothing in case the cold and darkness struck before they had finished their task — a very distinct possibility. They took with them prefabricated 'towns' which had every necessity for a prolonged stay, and whilst these 'towns' were quickly erected gangs of workers were busy laying lengths of cable back to the great powerhouses from where the basic energy would be generated. This, in turn, would be converted at each of the 'D-D' sites by the counter-apparatus itself.

Back and forth Holt flew, never sparing himself for a moment. His constitution stood up to it, but even he was not super-human, and ten days and nights of fiendish activity, almost without sleep and only with hurried meals, took their abrupt toll. He collapsed unexpectedly in the midst of a government meeting and had to be rushed to his home, there to lie suffering from complete nervous prostration.

Automatically the calm, indefatigable Luther took over. He knew the whole scheme and set-up so was well able to step into Holt's shoes. So, as the fourteen days began to run out, a kind of frenzy hit the world. In one direction it lay amongst the workers exclusively engaged on the 'Holt Rankin Project', and in the other it lay amongst the millions of ordinary folk who knew that the sands were running out that their leaders were waging a desperate battle against time to save the situation.

On the thirteenth night the skies, though cloudless, were also starless. It was an ominous, significant fact, and revealed the nearness of the onrushing darkness. The moon shone at the half phase, being, of course, millions of miles nearer Earth than any of the blacked-out stars. Towards two o'clock on the morrow the first onset of the darkness was calculated to become apparent.

The various governments put their emergency plans into operation, hampered considerably by their inability to use sound. Mass e-mails were sent out to those able to receive them, and in addition giant notices were posted up in strategic positions on the thirteenth evening, warning everybody to have their protective clothing handy. Again by e-mails ships were ordered to their nearest ports and airplanes were grounded. Long-distance trains were all cancelled and motor road services abandoned. Unless desperate necessity demanded it nobody was to move from the place where he or she at present abided. All naked lights were to be extinguished since, if the darkness proved to be all that was expected there would be no way to detect any fires which might break out.

The food stores of the world had long been organised. Every home had its official government stocks, and in every village, town and city in the world vast storehouses had been crammed with tinned and other edible goods that the great factories had been turning out. The world had been denuded of growing foodstuffs and it had all been gathered in and scientifically treated to withstand the awful conditions that would prevail, and in charge of these storehouses were the blind! The only persons who could possibly handle the distribution, they had all been briefed and stood ready.

Throughout the thirteenth night humanity shifted and moved, but generally obeyed instructions, and by dawn the whole world was mysteriously still, everybody waiting for the ultimate blow to fall. Or rather *almost* everybody. Those engaged on the Holt Rankin Project were still working like demons under their various overseers, with Luther supervising everything as near as possible. Some of the generators were already being installed and others were on their way by road and rail. What would happen when blackness descended nobody quite knew.

5

Darkness descends

To a certain extent, Holt had recovered, but he was definitely out of the running as far as organizing or controlling anything was concerned. Allowed only to rise from bed for short periods, Linda or a nurse in constant attendance upon him, he fumed and chafed over his inability to be present as events moved to the crisis. Linda indeed had all her work cut out to make him obey the doctor's orders. That he did so was only because he knew that Luther was to be relied upon to carry things through.

On the morning of the fourteenth day he rose after breakfast and insisted on dressing. This accomplished after considerable effort he moved into the lounge and took up position in the armchair where he could see through the French windows. Linda, acting on his instructions, brought the heavy protective furs into the room and laid them nearby, then she came and sat down silently beside him.

'From here,' he 'said', looking out into the bright morning, 'we'll have a grand-stand view of whatever is to happen . . . and it occurs to me that this lip-reading business we have so completely mastered isn't going to be any use in the dark. So we'd better use touch. Morse. You understand it?'

'I don't remember all the alphabet,' Linda confessed. 'I had to learn it as a girl guide in my school days, but that's a good way behind me now.'

'Then maybe I've time to refresh your memory. Give me your hand.'

Linda obeyed and for the next couple of hours, whilst they waited for the first manifestations of the darkness, Holt kept on repeating the Morse alphabet by finger pressure on Linda's hand until she had rubbed up much of her rusty knowledge concerning it. With time, of course, she would become proficient again.

At eleven o'clock Holt desisted, feeling unutterably weary again. Linda departed, fixed a beverage for both of them and then returned. She glanced towards the mantel-clock. Its pendulum, usually so noisy, was muted, even though it swung back and forth vigorously. The electric radiator glowed brightly for the autumn air had a chill. And everything was still silent, unutterably, deadly silent like the utter bowels of the deepest tomb.

Outside, the vision was like that of a dead planet. There was no wind and the dry grass in the garden, along with the autumn flowers, stood motionless. Not a soul in sight in the meadows beyond. No smoke from distant chimneys, for all naked lights had been expired. Into this category also came electric radiators, but Holt had his own reasons for having it on. He wished to see if heat radiation would fade in the manner anticipated.

And overhead the calm, dove-grey sky with a spot of white cloud drifting here and there. On a normal day it would have been glorious weather — sharply frosty, autumnal, yet well appropriate to the season.

By noon nothing had happened. The astronomers had said two o'clock, and there was no reason to doubt their mathematics. Linda again departed to prepare a lunch, all the time with a dead, hopeless feeling at the back of her brain, the gripping conviction that this might be the last meal she would ever prepare in the light. Unless the toilers on her husband's electrical project succeeded in the gigantic task he had set them before himself falling by the wayside.

With little more than understanding glances at each other they ate the lunch, dividing their attention between the view outside of the autumn midday and the clock on the mantelpiece By the time Linda had cleared everything away it was one-thirty. She returned to her chair, drew it close so that Holt could put his arm about her, then they sat watching — and waiting. As indeed all the world was watching and waiting at that moment, except the grim-faced engineers on the Project.

As far as this was concerned, everything was still going full blast — the foundries, the electrical manufacturers, the transport workers, and the men at the sites, and amidst it all was the ubiquitous Luther, paying no heed to the possible onset of darkness beyond an occasional glance at the sky. Three generators and projectors had been installed, which was something, but hundreds more had to follow to be placed in their predetermined sites in different parts of the world.

For Linda there was stirring a dim hope that perhaps the astronomers had been wrong, that her husband had been wrong, and that the core of the dyno-depressant would pass Earth by. For, when she stirred a little and glanced at the clock, it was 2.15, and still nothing had transpired. The view outside was unchanged. The room seemed a little colder than before, certainly, but —

'Holt!' she gasped soundlessly, and though he could not hear her he felt the fierce clutch she gave his arm. He moved his head and followed the direction of her gaze.

The electric fire was fading out! It was as though it had been switched off, the element dying from bright red to a dim glow and then expiring altogether. Might be the powerhouse, of course, under orders to cut off power . . . no, that could not be it. Power was to be left on for vital machinery if not for light or heat.

Holt stood stiffly to his feet and wandered into the hall to inspect the fuse box. It was quite in order. The power was on all right — the hall lights came up normally when he pressed the button — but the radiator was dead. He returned into the lounge, gave a brief glance at Linda's taut features and then inspected the radiator plug. Nothing wrong there, either. At length he left the plug out of its socket and held his hands to the element. Despite the fact that it had been on so very recently it was absolutely stone cold.

'Is it — it?' Linda's lips framed the words awkwardly.

'Afraid so.' Holt found it a queer reflection, but now, that the moment of crisis was upon him he felt a good deal stronger and ready to fight it. Such is the mysterious alchemy of the human structure when brought to the peak of resistance.

'But it's still light,' Linda's lips said, as she glanced about her and then outside.

'Heat waves and red waves are higher up the spectrum scale than the combination of waves which form light,' Holt replied, as scientific as ever. 'The red in the radiator element has blacked out, and so has the heat.'

He crossed to the window where the early afternoon sunlight was streaming in and stood in the direct rays for a moment or two. Then he gave a wry smile.

'No heat whatever,' he 'said' at last. 'Not even through the glass. Heat's gone, Linda. We'd better get into the furs.'

Feeling like one in a suicide pact Linda complied. In a matter of five minutes they were wrapped up like polar explorers, except that they had not yet drawn the hoods and facemasks into position. It seemed a ridiculous situation for, outside, the sun was shining and as yet the air was by no means really cold, though there certainly was a suggestion of chill.

'And now?' Linda's lips framed the words briefly, her eyes clearly showing the terror she was experiencing.

Holt motioned to the chairs again and they reseated themselves. They had hardly been settled for five minutes before there came an imperceptibly creeping twilight upon the face of things. At first it was so vague as to hardly be noticeable — a deepening of shadows, a darker aspect in the less bright corners, but as the time advanced it was inevitably forced upon both of them that light *was* dying in a very slow fade-out.

Linda made to half jump up in her alarm, but Holt grabbed her wrist in his gloved hand and forced her back into her chair. His gaunt, tired face was turned towards the windows, so Linda looked also — upon a countryside beyond the garden foundering gradually as though before the advancing shadow of a total eclipse. The phenomenon was particularly unnerving because, though the darkness was obviously descending the sun itself was shining brightly! The sky, though, was changing from blue to purple, shading into black as dust motes no longer transmitted their light photons.

In ten minutes the process, as far as the surface of the Earth was concerned, was complete. Holt and Linda sat motionless, stunned by the situation. Everything around them had a phantom-like quality and was barely perceptible — but absolute dark had not descended because the deluge of light-waves poured forth direct from the sun had not yet succumbed to the advancing D-D core. Everything else, using reflected light, had. The result was that all objects appeared as though seen by a half-moon — pale, unreal, somehow lost.

Holt shifted his head, wondering if he could explain something to Linda, but he knew it was impossible. Her face was a dim white circle upwardly turned to the black, starless sky. He wanted to tell her that the final act had not yet been played. The D-D core had 93-million miles further to travel before it embraced the sun. Then indeed it would be dark — the darkness of absolute non-sight.

Moving a little, Holt looked eastwards and peered towards a three-quarter moon, serene in the black heavens with only the sun for company. But at length it turned green, then blue, and finally faded out entirely as its light was cut off. So the advancing alien field swept onwards irresistibly to the central fount of the Solar System, and awe-stricken by the elemental force of it all, Holt, Linda, and countless millions of human beings watched for the last word to be written.

It came some ten minutes later, proving that the electrical field must be advancing at something approaching the speed of light — the natural speed of all electrical emanations. The first sign that it had reached the luminary came when the usual eye-searing brilliance of the photosphere became masked to a baleful red. It changed swiftly into orange and then it became yellow again. Linda breathed a little more rapidly, feeling that perhaps the sun was not going to founder after all. But Holt knew differently. The orb was merely descending the spectrum scale to extinction and changing colour as one wave after another bowed before the all-conquering dyno-depressant.

The yellow became a sickly, frightening green and painted the silent Earth with hellish shadows. So it shaded off into blue, as magnificent as a giant celestial sapphire.

Indigo — deep violet . . . An even deeper violet that wavered and shimmered as millions of eyes watched it. The limit of the visible spectrum had been reached. After violet — bar the invisible ultra-violet — there lay extinction, and into that lightless abyss the sun was fast declining.

Holt and Linda held tightly on to each other, watching the darkening cloak over the landscape, or else that violet blur high in the heavens.

It paled. It was difficult to see where it lay . . . Then it had gone. Silence. Darkness, utter darkness, lay over the face of the world. It brought everything to a standstill whilst men and women everywhere reacted to it. There had never been anything like it before. By itself it would have been terrifying, but with the added curse of utter silence it was beyond all toleration. No, not quite. There is far more character in the human make-up than is apparent in normal conditions, and in every direction there slowly began a rising urge to meet this thing, this affliction of Nature, to stand up to it at least until, perhaps, the Holt Rankin Project brought relief.

Holt felt something stir in the abyss and realised it was Linda's hand gripping his wrist and falteringly transmitting a Morse message.

'Are you still alive?'

'Quite alive, but stunned.'

'No more than I am. I never thought darkness could be intense. It hurts!'

In this Linda was correct. Everybody in the world, normally sighted, was finding the blackness to have a quality of pressure. Just as, at first, the Silence had hung like lead against the eardrums, so the dark now pressed on the eyeballs. And definitely was a darkness beyond description. Above, around, below, to those out in the open, there was no apparent difference. Everything was jet, and becoming colder and colder, as with warmth no longer functioning, what little stored-up heat there was in human bodies fast began to dissipate. Those in the temperate and frigid climates were not unusually disturbed by the rapid decline in temperature — but in the tropical regions it was yet one more hell added to the blackness and silence.

After a long interval Linda's hand tapped again. 'What do we do? Go on sitting here?'

'Why not? Nothing we can do. We know where the food is and we have a roof over our heads. It will probably rain later due to condensation.'

Linda was about to 'tap' that they would not hear it if it did, but she refrained, Things were bad enough without her adding emphasis to them. So she tapped another question:

'How far had your invention got before this dark came?'

'Last news I had was that the first generators and projectors were being installed. But that's only a fragment. I have planned for dozens of them in different parts of the world.'

'How will the engineers communicate now? Or see what to do with vital connections?'

'As to communication, they'll probably do as we are doing. Regarding the machine connections, they're stamped in relief numbers in readiness in case the darkness caught up. A sample was tried by a blind man and he worked perfectly by touch. It must be done soon, before hands become too cold.'

Luther, too, had added his own improvisations against the coming of the darkness, and he was still in control of the situation. At the final extinction of the sun's light he had been at the site of the North London projector — and here he still was, clad in his protective clothes and with an army of invisible and somewhat frightened helpers around him. He gave his orders by the Morse system, to men who had been trained beforehand to utilise it. Indeed, it had been one of the conditions of training that Morse must be learned — and now the reason was obvious.

The equipment itself was all stamped in embossed letters and numbers, most of them large enough to be felt through gloves, and specifications were duplicated in Braille so that blind experts first 'read' them and then 'tapped' them to Luther — or to whichever underling scientist was in charge of a particular site. The necessary wires were also tabulate with differing shaped discs or relief number-plates. In a word, everything had been designed so that it could be handled in the dark and the most intricate parts were handled by blind men or women whose skill was the outcome of years of practice in the sightless construction of radio and electronic equipment.

The most difficult matter of all was transport of the equipment from the source of manufacture. No lights would operate anywhere, and of course, driving was utterly impossible. Nor was there any radio or radar system that could function, either. The only possible way, which Luther lad fortunately foreseen, was to bring into action that willing friend of man — the horse! All of them sure-footed enough to find their way when led by men who had been over the routes in the light several scores of times accustoming themselves to the way.

No, man in his enterprise was not defeated even by the Dark, the Silence and the gradually deepening Cold. At the descent of the darkness the motor lorries stopped — most of them near to their depots since there had been ample warning of the fading light; then the horse-drawn drays and lorries, relics of a past age but now immeasurably useful, took over, led slowly but none the less surely along the Stygian highways.

This particular innovation as a means of transport was not limited to Britain. It was worldwide. In the frozen north dog-teams were used instead, but this was the only exception. From tropic to arctic 'blind' men and mainly genuinely blind animals added their quota, dragging the equipment from the nearest base.

In the factories themselves, dotted about all over the world, there could have been chaos but for the careful preliminary planning. Since all the machinery was preset there was no particular difficulty. Even when the Dark came the machinery carried on as normal, following its appointed mechanics and turning out the self-same article to pattern every time. In the assembly rooms the normal sighted staff was now in the hands of blind experts, being shown exactly what to do by touch instead of vision.

Concentrated effort, meticulous care, and above all unswerving courage: these were the virtues that continued to steer Mankind in his effort to defeat the dyno-depressant.

And, little by little, one by one, powerhouse after powerhouse was linked up to the projectors — men spreading out across the abysmal distances, feeling at the cables, masked to the ears in furs against the slowly intensifying Cold.

Cold! This was the greatest enemy of all, perhaps. The failure of heat waves did not mean instant freezing, for the process of heat dissipation proved to be more gradual than that of night-neutralisation, which had been cut off completely. In the case of heat the effect was similar to that of an oven from which the heat has been cut off. A steady cooling — and in the case of the Earth's surface certain rocks and areas kept their heat within themselves, mysteriously insulated, without radiating it in the normal way. Thus the Cold was slow in its development, but none the less inevitable.

Before the onset of the Cold there came the rain, the inevitable result of condensation. There was something maddening about it — a pitiless, soundless deluge beating out of the utter Darkness. It swamped the struggling men and animals on the roads, it washed out some of the highways completely, and in several instances rivers burst their banks and hurled a soundless torrent over the land, coming without warning and wiping out everything in the track. During this period the workers on the Rankin Project were very much like ants under the impact of a hosepipe stream. They were flung in all directions, drowned, maimed, buried under the vehicles they were guiding, overwhelmed in an utter blackness and silence from which the deluge battered relentlessly.

This condition lasted for three normal days and nights and then as suddenly changed to wet snow, and as suddenly again to freezing rain. Smothered to the ears in their furs and with protective helmets over their heads and faces, the gallant army of men and women fought the most impossible conditions to get the projectors erected one by one. Luther, tireless as ever, had 'runners' constantly on the move between one projector station and another, keeping him posted as to progress. And as fast as each projector station was completed and linked up to the nearest powerhouse the energy was released into the all-pervading blackness. There was no means of telling whether the equipment was working correctly for no sound could be heard and no meters could be seen. It was absolute blind chance in every case. But despite the fact that half-a-dozen projectors were in action there was no sign of the D-D being destroyed, even though Holt had said that the merest upset in the balance would destroy the entire alien field.

Luther found himself wondering about this. If the smallest electrical charge into the whole mass could bring about dissipation, why the need for so many projectors ringing the Earth? He had meant to question Holt upon this point, but his collapse had prevented it. Actually, the reason was explainable enough. Each projector only emitted a very slight voltage — as compared to the colossal load of the D-D field — and Holt had worked out mathematically just how much power would be needed, the minimum amount, to produce the desired effect on the D-D field. Rather than concentrate all the power into one projector, which would have been impossible because of the load, he had split it up over many machines and placed them so that each one struck the field at a different part of the Earth's surface, thereby making sure that equal power would be produced *outwards* from all sides.

Luther thought once of making an effort to contact Holt, and then decided against it. To find his way in the utter darkness would be next to impossible, and besides he was wanted constantly at the power-site that he had made his headquarters. Men and women were constantly applying to him in Morse for advice, instructions, and direction.

Holt himself, on the other hand, was finding it less and less possible to stay put in the house, feeling his way around, 'tapping' conversations with Linda, eating and sleeping and hoping for results. It was a case of his mental anxiety overruling his physical weakness following his illness, for he told himself he was quite capable of being back on the job helping to control the scientific experiment he had set in motion. To have no word, no sight of anything, no sound or suggestion of how things were faring was become beyond toleration.

'I've got to take a risk and find out what is going on,' he 'told' Linda, a week after the Dark had descended. 'We sit around here, smothered up like Eskimos, blind and deaf to the world, and out there somewhere my protectors are being put up. Or at least I hope so. I've got to know!'

'You can't,' Linda 'morsed' back to him.

'I've been thinking out how perhaps I can. I know the exact location of all the projector sites, since I measured up the distances myself. The nearest power-site is North London, a distance of about five miles from here. I've more than a mind to try and reach it.'

'In this! Don't be crazy, Holt!'

His fingers tapped back urgently: 'It isn't crazy! Don't you realise that if anything has gone wrong the engineers, or Luther, won't be able to communicate with me? I've far more chance of finding the solitary projector-site than they have of finding this house in a suburban region. Besides, I cannot stay here any longer, wondering — wondering.'

Long pause. 'Could I come with you? I'd be scared to death to stay in this.'

'By all means. I did not suggest it because I thought it would be too much for you. North London, and the site, lies to the right of here, and I know the terrain pretty well. Mainly meadowland, and I've a good mental impression of the landscape. What I propose to do is take a reel of very fine wire with us. I've got about a mile of it in the outhouse, stuff left over from transformer windings, It will give us a lifeline back to the house if after the first mile we find things too intolerable. How about it?'

'I'm game. I'll fix some food and drink to take with us.'

On this they parted — Linda to the kitchen regions and Holt to the outhouse. He discovered when he opened the back door, for the first time since the Darkness, just what sort of conditions would have to be faced. A gale-force wind stumbled him backwards for a moment and Linda, only a little distance away, feeling around the kitchen table, also felt the fury of the elements. But neither of them sensed the cold; their furs prevented it. Except on their faces, since they were not wearing helmets. Here they sensed the razor-wind, full of the frigid breath of deep winter.

Not that it deterred Holt. He dragged up the cowl of his fur coat over his head and plunged down the steps into the abyss. Snow was round his legs. He could feel it soddening his trouser legs and pulling him back with every step he took. By the time he had fumbled his way to the outhouse he was stiff with cold and his snow-caked legs and feet were numb.

With aching fingers he groped around for the reel of wire, found it at last, and began the blind man's stumbling way back to the house. Not the faintest gleam of light showed anywhere, Just the total abyss, a blackness blacker than blindness itself.

He stumbled over the steps at last and found his way into the kitchen again, closing the door. The air inside was not much warmer, but at least the biting wind was shut off. He felt around again until at last he contacted Linda. With his chilled fingers he gave her warning.

'Temperature's down well below freezing from the feel of it, and there's no chance of it ever climbing again until the D-D is destroyed. It will keep on going down. We'll both need gumboots and our helmets. To say nothing of the gloves.'

All these had been provided by the government so they donned them; then with the haversack of provisions over his shoulder — though he had no conception when it would be possible to eat any of them — Holt led the way out of the

French windows, made sure Linda was with him, and then locked the windows behind him, fastening the end of his life line wire to the window knob.

This done they began their journey across the garden, more or less familiar, except that the snow made the normal ground level difficult to follow. They lost track of lawn and flowerbeds and just kept going until they collided with the fence.

Here they stopped for a moment in this gale-ridden, blizzard-plastered blackness. They could feel the intensity of the wind, but it did not penetrate their furs and facemasks. For all they knew their masks were probably plastered in snow. It was impossible to tell. Certainly the air-vents were getting blocked for they found breathing difficult and had to smear their gloved hands over the vents at intervals to keep the orifices clear.

After considerable difficulty the fence was negotiated, Holt taking care not to get his lifeline wire entangled with it. Then, knowing they were facing the meadows, and the unknown, he paused for a moment with a hand on Linda's arm, weighing up which was 'right' from the position in which they now stood.

'It's a long chance — maybe a hopeless gamble.' Linda felt his gloved hand tapping the message on her arm. 'But at least we are doing something and that's better than sitting still. Right! Let's go.'

Linda left it to him, clinging on to his arm. In the hand of his other arm he allowed the wire drum to spin gently. So, gradually, they advanced in the raging dark, having to feel with their feet for every inch of the way. They found themselves in ditches, mixed up with hedges that seemed to have no way round them, and all the time there was the buffeting, soundless wind, the sense of snowflakes whirling even though they could not be seen, and the eternal dark and silence. It seemed now an incredible feat of imagination to grasp that this was the same countryside in which, in the past, they had spent many a picnic — a quiet, meadowland region between the suburb in which they lived and the great area of the metropolis.

On and on, with not the least conception of whether they were on the right track or not. It was when it seemed they must have been floundering for nearly two hours that Linda dragged to a halt, her hand on Holt's arm speaking her thoughts.

'We're just not getting anywhere, Holt! Let's start going back. We should never have attempted it.'

'Can't go back now.'

'Why not? You've got the lifeline there, haven't you?'

'Not any more: It came to an end nearly an hour ago, so suddenly I didn't have time to catch at it before it was lost. That must have been when we'd covered the first mile. I didn't mention it because I didn't want to scare you.'

'Which means we've lost the way back home? That we're stuck out here with no idea where we are or where we're going?'

Long pause; then, 'Yes.'

Even longer pause from Linda before her gloved hand tapped again. 'Then we may as well fold up right here and finish! We can't go on — '

'We can, and we're going to. I'm convinced we're in the right direction. In any case where's the sense of stopping and giving up the ghost when by an effort we might find our way? We can't get back, so let's go forward, until the finish.'

Linda did not answer, but the fact that she began moving again was sufficient evidence for Holt that she was still willing to try and see the mad venture through.

6

The return of heat

MAD was right! The further they groped and stumbled into the darkness the fiercer the hurricane seemed to become, until they were bending before it, dragging their snow-caked legs with infinite difficulty, wearily keeping the air-vents clean and sucking in atmosphere which was so thin and biting it cut the throat and lungs.

They both realised there was a limit to what they could stand, that they had probably committed suicide in their effort to conquer the merciless conditions. The more this conviction grew on Linda, the more the silence and the dark weighed on her consciousness, the less effort she put forth. And at last she fell, not caring, wanting only to sleep and forget this blind arctic hell into which she and Holt had come.

'Lin!' She could feel Holt's hand

banging at signals on her arm. 'Get up! To give up in this is fatal. It's the thin, heady atmosphere which is doing it — Get a grip on yourself!'

Linda yawned inside her helmet but made no effort to move. At which Holt dragged her fiercely to her feet and shook her violently until something of the stupor cleared from her senses. She started walking again mechanically, then both she and Holt fell over at the same moment, tripping over some object buried deep in the snow.

The collapse was entirely sufficient for Linda. She did not intend to get up again without extremely good reason. But for Holt there was a different purpose. He felt around for the cause of the fall they had made, convinced from the brief contact his feet had made with the object that it was some kind of a pipe, and he knew very well that no pipe existed in the meadow area which they were still presumably covering.

Impatiently he groped about him, until his gloved hand abruptly encountered the object. It *was* a pipe! Risking the cold he tugged off one of his gloves and felt the object circumspectly, feeling his fingers become brittle and numb as he did so. Within a few seconds he had identified the object and felt around for Linda, shaking her savagely. That she moved in his grip satisfied him that she was still conscious.

'We can't miss now, Lin! We can't miss! We've stumbled on one of the cables from projector to powerhouse! Following it one way or the other we're bound to come to shelter.'

Linda awakened a little. 'Cable? Lying loose?'

'All there was time for. They were carried from projectors to powerhouses across the landscape like wire over a studio floor. No time for pylons or subterranean channels. We can really get somewhere if we follow it.'

This was enough to get Linda struggling to her feet again. Holt returned his glove to his hand and helped her, then using the buried cable as their guide, kicking it as they went to make sure it was there, they plunged again into the welter of wind and invisible plastering snow.

They must have been much nearer to one end of the cable than they had imagined, for not ten minutes later they collided with a solid wall. Almost immediately they began to feel their way around it until they came to the outline of something they took to be a door. Holt felt for the latch, discovered it, then tried to move it. To his overwhelming relief it finally moved, but he had to knock away caked ice to make it operate. Very carefully he crept forward into the void, Linda clinging on behind him. No use calling out. No use doing anything to announce their presence . . . Then he bumped into something, and it moved. Another person!

He gripped tightly, using Morse in the hope it would be understood.

'Where are we? I have my wife with me. Is this a powerhouse or a projector site? It must be one or the other.'

'North London projector site,' came the efficient Morse answer. 'Let me shut the door: the wind's cutting us in two.'

A sense of movement, the collision of

other people, and then the Morse tappings resumed on Holt's arm.

'That's better! We're fairly comfortable in here as long we wear our furs; but we're not using our masks and hoods, which is why I noticed the wind. Who are you? Where the devil have you come from in these ghastly conditions?'

'I am Holt Rankin, and my wife is right beside me. I felt I must make the attempt. I'd never have made it but for falling over your main power cable. Where's Dr. Luther?'

'Here, in this projector site. This is wonderful, Mr. Rankin! We've been racking our brains to decide how to get in touch with you. Here, you need rest. Hang on to me, both of you.'

Holt did as he was ordered and Linda automatically moved with him. By degrees they found themselves down into chairs, then the tapping resumed.

'I'm chief engineer Halliday. I'll tell Dr. Luther. He's around here somewhere. You can take off your helmets if you want. It's cold in here but not intolerable.'

With that the chief engineer moved

away and Holt and Linda followed out his suggestion to remove their helmets. It was a relief to be able to breathe more or less normally, even though the air was cold, but otherwise nothing was changed. The Dark still pressed down on the eyes and the Silence upon the cars.

Then Holt realised a different hand was touching his own. He had removed his gloves and he realised the powerful masculine strength in the grip he received. A brief tapping assured him that it was Luther.

'If ever there were two people with courage it must be you two,' his signalling said. 'Risking that black, snow-buried hell outside — But I'm afraid you have only run from one trouble into another one,'

Holt felt his nerves tauten. 'Why? What's wrong?'

'Snow! What few runner-messengers I have left keep arriving with reports of snow bogging down our efforts of every hand. The transports can't get through. Horses are slipping down and staying that way. Men and equipment are being buried — I tell you, Rankin, we're in the devil's own mess. Of the hundred projector sites we have fixed, only about half of them have been equipped and started up. How we're going to finish the chain I don't know.'

Holt was motionless, thinking the matter out. He felt Linda's hand making enquiry, so he outlined briefly how things stood. He could feel Luther near to him, waiting.

'Is this station in operation?' Holt asked finally.

'Yes. It was one of the first to start up. So are the odd forty-seven or eight that have been completed since. But we're fighting a losing battle against these climatic conditions. It isn't as though we had light to be able to help those who are being overwhelmed. We're completely helpless, being driven to a standstill.'

'Powerhouses all right, from where the loads are being generated?'

'So the runners tell me. I've got the runners working like relay racers. They are strung in a chain throughout the world one passing a message to the other. Damned long winded method, I know

— and I'm right out of touch where oceans intervene. But where I've dry land connection I'm told that every power site we put up is working normally. Can't guarantee they'll go on doing so, though.'

'Why not?'

'The cold, man! Powerhouses need attention, no matter how automatically they run these days. And with the ever-dropping temperature, lack of warmth, impossibility of hot food or drinks, the poor devils of humans running them will break down and die. Then the powerhouses will stop.' Pause as Luther seemed to reflect; then his signalling resumed. 'We're up against it in earnest, Rankin, and I think we're beaten. Ask yourself: How long do you think you can stand these ghastly conditions? The Silence, yes. Even the Dark. But the awful cold — that gets you in the end.'

Holt knew the scientist was right. With every minute now the cold was becoming more intense. Those few vestiges of heat radiations, which had remained, mysteriously insulated and dissipating their beneficence only by degrees, were about extinct. The thermometer mercuries must be plummeting down. Already, despite the thick furs, Holt, Linda, Luther, and the few men gathered in this projector site, could detect the numbing of their extremities. They were in an infinitely worse position than Arctic explorers. They could not speak to each other, could not huddle round a paraffin stove, could not even see. It was a prospect sufficient to crush the last spark of hope in the strongest heart.

Then Luther resumed a communication: 'I wanted to contact you to find out if it signifies if we only work with half the required number of projectors. Does that make the whole effort useless?'

'According to mathematics, yes.' There was an aching despair in Holt's heart as he tapped a message back. 'Mathematics say we need the full load to achieve the repulsive balance I am striving at. Sometimes, though, things don't work out in practice as they do in theory. Maybe half the load, which seems to be all we can count on as things are, *might* do the trick.'

Luther asked a significant question:

'Then why hasn't it? We've been on half power for over a week now, but nothing's happened. I think we've got to admit ourselves beaten, Rankin. The powerhouses will soon come to a stop, and the projector sites can never be completed.'

In this he spoke an absolute truth. Had somebody with the blessed gift of being able to see in the dark been able to take a swift world tour he would have seen that on the highways assigned to the Rankin Project there lay the smashed and dying remnants of his grand ambition. Lorries and drays lay overturned in the fast-burying blizzard. Horses were dead and frozen solid, their human guides motionless under the weight of the everlasting avalanche from above. Out in the screaming dark lay ruin. The Rankin Project could never be finished.

Of the hundred planned projector-sites only forty-seven had been completed and were in operation. For a week they had emanated D-D energy into the core of the dyno-depressant itself, without the least apparent vestige of effect. Soon, as the watchers of the powerhouses died with the cold and exposure, this power too would cease, to leave an ice-bound world, dark, silent, lost — until perhaps at some unforeseeable date the alien energy chanced to pass by. If it ever did . . . Holt remembered how it had yawned way back into the light-centuries beyond the Milky Way.

He stirred a little, found Luther's hand and signalled. 'We need food, my wife and I. Maybe we can think better then. We have some provisions with us, so we won't take yours.'

'I wish there were hot drinks. Heat of any kind at all would help. But that's gone too.'

Holt pulled the rucksack from his shoulder and felt within it, handling the dry, cold-hard sandwiches to Linda beside him for her to take the first share. She did so. They ate them and drank water that was only thawed out by the warmth of Holt's back where the rucksack had lain against it. After this had been done there did not seem anything else to do, except sit, and shiver, and try to think. Luther was still close at hand,

Holt realised. He could sense his nearness, and his outreaching hand presently contacted him.

'How many people are in this site altogether?' Holt asked.

'Eight — including you and your wife.'

'Which means you have only provisions for six, and now we come and plant ourselves upon you. It won't do, Luther. We ought to try and find our way back home.'

'You'd never make it. And you know it.'

'Yes, I know it,' Holt tapped back. 'It would not matter much, anyway. Since we've failed there's no point in — '

He did not finish his sentence because somebody abruptly collided with him. Immediately hands gripped his shoulders in a movement that was steadying and suggested apology — then as Holt recovered himself and wondered what was happening it occurred to him that somebody had evidently entered the site from outside. There was still the frigid, arctic blast of the wind sweeping across his face from where the door had been left open. It ceased abruptly as somebody evidently closed it.

Then came Luther's hand, again quickly communicating.

'One of my runners has managed to get through from the North London power-house, and he tells me nobody's alive there. The men in charge are lying on the floor motionless — or at least in the snow covering the floor. The Braille detector shows that the machinery has ceased operating. That means this projector has too.'

Holt was becoming inured to smashing shocks. He tapped a question: 'How many projectors were fed by North London?'

'Four. Which means every one of them must be out of action. Only a question of time before the others go.'

Holt thought for a while, then: 'We have only one hope — and a very slim one. Namely, that the charge we've injected into the D-D field may have a delayed action effect, just as a thunder-storm doesn't break until it reaches a certain potential. Maybe I'm saying it to cheer us up, but it's possible, and therefore nothing will happen until a certain potential level is reached, enough to disturb the D-D field and cause it to break down. It doesn't conform with my mathematics, I know, but I cannot guarantee that they were accurate, anyway, because the D-D is a field of which we know little from the mathematical side. I do insist though that the charge we've been pouring into the D-D for over a week must have done something, even if it was only half of what I'd intended.'

'In another twenty-four hours — or less — it won't matter to us whether there is a delayed action or not: the cold will have got us by then. For myself,' Luther finished, 'I'm going to try and get some sleep, and I hope to God I never wake up again.'

His hand moved away and Holt was left with the realisation that at last Luther had admitted himself beaten. He had done all he knew — and failed.

'What is going on, Holt?' came Linda's questioning hand. 'Was that a messenger who came in?'

Holt gave her the details and could imagine her expression when he had finished.

'Then — then what do we do now? There must be some other move, surely?'

'None. We have done everything and we're right at the end of the road.'

Linda moved restlessly. 'I'm not going to sit here and freeze to death, Holt. Besides, we have no guarantee that whoever else is here with us will take it quietly — the inevitability of death, I mean. If one of them should go off the deep end I don't want to be involved in it.'

'I had thought of the same thing. I'd already told Luther we might try and find our way back home. Probably we never will, but it might be better to meet death out there, you and I together, than mixed up with this lot.'

Since both their minds were made up there was no longer any hesitation in their actions. They both got to their feet. Holt shouldering the rucksack — though he felt he would never have to use it again — and then they picked their way carefully forward towards the source of the icy draught they had felt when the messenger had come in.

Holt found it without much difficulty and pulled it open. Instantly the icy wind blasted inwards, but this time there was no snow — no rain, no anything on his face or Linda's as they quickly drew their helmets into place. Then, before any hands could reach out and restrain them they were on the outside of the door, closing it behind them.

They were conscious of two things as they stood in the dark and tried in vain to get their bearings for the way home. One thing was that the gale had dropped to a breeze, and that their feet were on firm but slippery ground. No longer soft snow that had plunged them up to their knees. There was one other thing, too — the deadly cold which was seeping even through their furs, and most certainly attacking their gloved hands and heavily-shod feet.

Linda hoped for a wild moment that this was a change for the better, and the very hope gave her the necessary energy to start walking in the darkness with Holt beside her. For him there was no such optimism. He knew exactly what had happened. The last traces of warmth had gone which, in conflict with the cold, had produced the condensation — first the rain and then the snow. Now the temperature had equalised at a considerable depth below zero, a temperature probably remaining level to the limit of the atmosphere. Consequently the wind had ceased also, there being no more disturbed air currents. All that remained was the pitiless, ever-intensifying frost that had already hardened the fallen snow to the toughness of granite.

In one sense it made the going easier, but in another it had destroyed any possible landmarks that they might have found useful. Or did it matter? The whole effort to try and reach home again was sheer suicide, and in their innermost hearts they knew it.

And yet they kept on going, drawn by the feeling that sooner or later they would strike something which would give them some clue as to how to return to their starting point. When they did find this 'clue', if such it could be called, it was not anything they could have foreseen. Both of them found themselves unexpectedly in a small, knee-high trench, its sides as hard and slippery as those of a glacier. More for the sake of it than anything else they kept on following it, finding it easier than the slippery, dangerous terrain that had no supporting 'walls' on either side.

Then it suddenly came to Holt where they were and what they were doing. He came to a standstill, gripping Linda's arm and then signalling.

'This is a stroke of luck we didn't bargain for! This is the trench we made through the snow on the outward journey! In the meantime half of it has filled in, which makes it knee-deep at the moment and frozen solid. I suppose we can thank the high wind which stopped the snow from filling things up to a very great depth.'

'Which means we might possibly follow it back home?' came Linda's quick question.

'No reason why not, if we can last out that long. Let's carry on and see.'

They moved on again, their movements the only thing keeping them from being overcome by the appalling cold. They reckoned that they ought eventually to come to the cable which had been the means of leading them to the projector-site, until it dawned on Holt that since the trench was half-filled in the cable must be buried under the ice.

There seemed no reason to suppose, cable or no cable that they would not finally land back home if they could only keep in the track of the trench. The snow had levelled the whole countryside, and they were the only two people who had travelled in it.

They managed to keep in the trail, despite the difficulties of the darkness and the glacial state of the ice. At times they lost track, which resulted in a frantic searching, then they could pick up the slippery hollow and carry on. Thus wise they mounted half-buried hedges and fences, obstacles that they remembered from the outward journey.

The trip seemed endless, and the cold maddening in its intensity; but there came a time at last when they found a fairly tall, familiar fence blocking their progress. Holt felt cautiously around it, endeavouring to identify it, and in the process his gloved hands became snarled up with a length of wire.

'We're there!' Linda felt his hand tapping her arm urgently. 'I've just come across that lifeline wire.' Nothing to stop us finishing the job within a few seconds.'

They struggled over the fence and dropped to the ice-caked garden beyond. Thereafter it was only a matter of following the wire back to the lounge French windows. Here they encountered unexpected difficulty since a brief groping around told them that the windows were buried in ice, or at least frozen snow, up to half their length. Holt did the only thing possible — smashed them in — and then helped Linda after him into the lounge. Here, though the darkness was still utterly unrelieved, they felt a little happier since they were feeling objects that were at once familiar.

'Wait a moment whilst I cover the windows up with the curtains,' Holt signalled. 'Might as well stop as much of the cold as possible from getting in.'

Linda waited for him beside the table, removing her helmet and face mask. Immediately the stinging air whipped her cheeks but it was preferable to the mask's stuffy interior. Then Holt was back, his cold, ungloved hand tapping hers.

'We've done a good deal to be thankful for, though how much use it will be to us in the long run I don't know. Best thing we can do is have something more to eat and drink — or we'll consume frozen water in place of drinking the real thing — and then we can try and get some sleep. The more sleep we can get the less we'll need in provisions. I need hardly tell you that those we have got are all we're likely to have . . . '

Linda hardly needed reminding of the fact, but as far as she could remember the kitchen was pretty well stocked. She had indulged in quite a deal of 'panic' buying before this darkness had settled down, just as had everybody else as far as the authorities would allow. This was in addition to the government allowance that had been distributed.

She scrambled together the meal,

smashed icicles from the cold water tap for drinking, and fumbled her way back into the lounge. Thus, in the utter dark and silence, she and Holt sat next to each other, still muffled in their furs, long since accustomed to having no sensation in their feet and legs and hardly any in their fingers. When the meal was over they felt slightly warmer, but this was the only amelioration in the otherwise impossible situation.

'If we go to sleep in this deadly cold, there's no real guarantee that we'll ever wake up, is there?' Linda's icy hand questioned.

'None at all — but does it matter? Surrounded with all the manifestations of the end of the world and the death of the human race I can't see it signifies — and sleep we must have. Nature will see to that.'

'I just wondered if, by keeping awake as long as possible we might not still be rewarded by seeing this awful, catastrophe pass away. Deep down I haven't lost hope even yet.'

'That's only because you're not a

scientist, Lin. For myself, I believe that if anything were going to happen it would have done so by now — which reminds me: I just wonder what time it is? We seem to have done the devil of a lot. It was ten in the 'morning' when we set out.'

He rose to his feet, found his way to the mantelpieces and then felt around with numbed hands for the clock. It was the only one in the house which was any use in the present circumstances — an eight-day, pendulum mechanism with a front which opened down its entire length and the figures on the dial strongly relieved, making them readable to the touch.

Gently, Holt felt at the dial, his left hand resting flat, palm downwards, in the base of the clock so he could not perhaps dislodge it in his 'reading' activities. He had just determined that the time was 4.20 when it occurred to him that there was something unusual about the time-piece, something affecting the back of his left hand.

Warmth! *Warmth!* There was no doubt

about it. It was mainly noticeable because his hands were so bitterly cold. But warmth in a world from which heat radiation had gone? Probably some nervous reaction of his own. Even intense cold cannot be distinguished from heat under normal conditions.

He turned quickly and found his way back to Linda, still seated at the table. In a series of quick signals he made the position clear to her and in response she followed him to the clock and laid her own hands in the base of it, just below the free swing of the pendulum. After a moment or two she tapped a communication.

'I can feel a sort of warmth, too, though how much of it is real and how much imagination I don't know.'

Holt's signals came back: 'It won't be noticeable now because the front's been open some little while. Wait while I close it up for a space and then we'll try again. Don't put your hand under cover of any sort. Let them get as cold as possible: that will make them all the more sensitive to warmth if there is any.'

Linda did as she was told, reflecting that she could hardly become much colder anyway; but back of her mind she was deeply impressed by the possibilities of this phenomenon of warmth, if it really existed. Anxiously she waited.

Finally Holt nudged her again, which was sufficient for her to realise that she was expected to once more put her hands into the clock. She did so — and this time there was no doubt about it; a definite warmth was present. Immediately she signalled Holt quickly with her free left hand.

'Try it quickly. It just can't be imagination!'

He responded promptly enough, then after a pause in which she could feel him close beside her, Linda felt him communicate again.

'Come over to the table and sit down. There's no doubt that something wonderful has happened!

They found their way back to their former positions and Holt began a long and laborious communication.

'Heat waves have been the most

unstable radiations right from the start. Remember how they lingered in some inanimate things even after everything else had become 'blacked out'? Now it seems they are the first to make a reappearance. Reappearance, Lin! Think what that means!'

'I am doing,' she signalled back. 'But what has made it happen, and why on earth should it be warm inside that clock?'

'It's warm inside the clock because everything else is so devilishly cold outside it. A clock like that, with springs to operate its pendulum, has a good deal of potential energy stored up within it. Normally the dissipation thereof — which also causes the pendulum to swing — would never be noticed, but because everything else is cold we can definitely detect the faint aura of warmth created by the slight energy being dissipated. Put more simply it is the warmth of friction. As to the reason for it, there can only be one: the dyno-depressant field is starting to weaken!'

Linda felt her heart leap. 'But, Holt,

you said you'd given up all hope of it!'

'So I had, when nothing happened — but as I told Luther there exists a chance that a balance may be found by the energy already impregnated into the D-D field. It begins to look as though that has actually happened. At least it appears that heat waves are actually functioning again — The clock is not much of a test. We must try fire!'

'Dangerous, isn't it, when we shan't be able to see or hear it?'

'I'm going to try and light one in the grate, where the radiator at present stands — '

'Come to think of it,' Linda's tapping hand interrupted, 'why doesn't the radiator start giving off warmth if heat waves have come back? It isn't doing — or at least I can't feel it.'

'For two reasons. One because I left it unplugged, and the other because the North London powerhouse is out of action, and it is from there that we draw our energy. I'm going to get it away from the coal fire grate where it stands now and light a normal fire — if I can. Then we'll see!'

There was no more thought in their minds about sleep; there was no thought of anything except to test the validity of the apparent miracle which had come about. Holt got to his feet again, drew on his hood and gloves, and then made his way into the kitchen. After considerable difficulty he got the back door open and went out on to the glacier that led to the outhouse. He remembered there was some chopped wood in there, and some coal. He rarely used the old-fashioned style of fire, preferring the electric radiator, but here was a case where 'primitive' method had the advantage.

Before very long he was back in the lounge, to discover that in the interval Linda had done her share by removing the radiator. She was close beside him, he realised as he laid first paper and then wood in the grate, doing it very carefully, feeling meticulously before every move. At last he added the coal and then fumbled in his pocket for matches. The cold air bit around him as he had to unfasten his furs to perform this feat.

He found his matches at last and struck

one. Not a vestige of light or sound. Only the throat-catching odour of the sulphur as the smoke wafted under his nose. He hesitated a moment, absorbing a wonderful fact. The match flame, though invisible, was giving out normal heat! Gently he found the centre of the papers in the fire grate and released the match.

No sound. No light. That was the maddening part. The Dark and the perpetual Silence. But there was warmth. It could be felt shafting outwards and upwards, and with the seconds it increased. After the fiendish, deadening cold it was akin to the cessation of excruciating toothache.

Linda relaxed on the rug, soaking in the glorious warmth, drawing deep breaths of it, content for the time being that she could not see or hear just as long as the warmth would not desert her.

Her wish was realised. The seconds became minutes and the warmth still poured forth — in even greater measure as the fire presumably got well alight. Holt pictured what it must look like — the leaping flames, the glowing coal, the plumes of grey smoke sweeping up into the chimney shaft, He laid hold of the scientific fact that if heat waves could return like this it meant that other radiations could too. There might be stubborn resistance with certain of the wavelengths, but sooner or later, since the dyno-depressant field was obviously losing its grip, the whole unnatural terror must dissolve.

With all truth heat radiations *had* returned — all over the world. Frozen humanity had become conscious of this in varying ways in the past few hours, and the predominant fact was that it meant surcease from the damnable frigidity which had come close to extinguishing the whole human race. There was also another radiation that had returned — radio waves, one higher in the spectrum scale than heat waves, but nobody was aware of this because no power was yet operating anywhere in the world by which messages could be transmitted or received.

The return of heat radiations was, fortunately, gradual, otherwise the impact of normal warmth on the arctic cold might have produced electrical storms of inconceivable violence, if they could have been seen or heard. Even so there was extreme danger in the return of natural heat. The sun, though blacked out in the lightwave radiation, was in action again as far as its heat was concerned. Temperature was rising everywhere. The great plateaus of frozen snow and glacial ice were turning wet — and therein lay trouble.

Thaw — and inevitable flood!

7

Suicide pact

The world-wide consequences of the return of warmth were not matters which concerned either Holt or Linda as they absorbed the pleasure of a warm fire, both of them lying on the rug close by the heat and loosening their furs from about them. They underwent the tortures of cramp as frozen blood vessels started to function again, but this too they calmly accepted, their relief outweighing their pains.

Holt knew perfectly well that if heat radiations were operating here they must also be operating everywhere else in the world. Obviously the phenomenon could not be limited to this one room in a North London suburb, but he was so sleepy with reaction, so blissfully content in the realisation that the D-D was being beaten, that he did not foresee the possibility of a new menace in the form of fast thawing ice. He might have done had he heard the ice cracking on the windows as the temperature outside rose steadily under the late afternoon warmth of the sun — but of course there was no sound. No light. All the conditions were conducive to sleep. He began to tap a message to Linda as he felt that she was lying close by him.

'For us both to go to sleep might be a fatal mistake. One must stay awake to keep the fire under control, and to feed it. You take the first spell of sleep, and I'll do the second.'

Linda could only muster sufficient wakefulness to tap the word 'Right!' and then she had drowsed off, leaving Holt fighting a battle with himself to stop following her example. Somehow he stuck to his guns, putting pieces of coal on the fire at intervals — but now the warmth was becoming as unbearable as the cold had been, until at length it occurred to him that the temperature outside was perhaps rising fast as well, thereby warming the air in every direction.

He went to the French windows and

pulled aside the curtains. Stepping through the broken framework, cautiously to avoid any glass cuts, he found his feet sinking into wet slush. A soft, warm wind was blowing out of the black silence. It was so gentle, so caressing, it made him smile in silent joy to himself. There was no need to keep the fire going. The outside temperature was fast returning to normal.

He returned to where Linda was lying and settled beside her, feeling around for a spare cushion from the chesterfield with which to make a pillow. It was his intention to lie on guard, but Nature decided otherwise — and the next thing he knew was that his nostrils were filled with the unpleasant odour of a doused fire and that he was lying in shallow water. Evidently Linda had discovered the fact at the same moment for she was stirring beside him.

'What's happened?' her tapping hand demanded.

'Must be melted snow coming in and flooding the lower rooms. It's put the fire out anyway — We'd better get to an upstairs room quickly. The 'observatory' for preference.'

The 'observatory' was the small extra room that Holt had added to the house's upper level. It projected eight feet beyond the house wall and had two big windows and a glass roof, rather akin to an artist's studio. Within it Holt kept all his scientific tackle and records, together with a small but powerful telescope for astronomical work.

He got up, helped Linda to rise, and then groped around for the precious clock. With it in his hand he turned back to the girl.

'We'll need food in case we might get marooned. A flood is possible with all this ice and snow melting.'

'Right. I'll get some. You carry on. I can find my way up to the observatory easily enough.'

'I'll take the furs too. We may need them as night comes and the sun's warmth ceases.'

As night comes! Linda laughed hollowly to herself. It had been nothing else but rayless night for as long as she could remember. She had become as accustomed to it as though total blindness — and deafness — had descended upon her, and inwardly marvelled that she had the courage to override both and still keep on struggling. Only the return of heat — and hope — had given her new courage. This much she knew. The hope that the blessed hour would yet come when normality would return.

So she floundered out into the kitchen regions, and found she was defending her face against the chilling jets of water spurting from burst pipes. Drenched, ankle deep in water, she felt her way to the cupboard where she had stocked the various provisions.

Meanwhile Holt gathered together the furs — fortunately on the chesterfield clear of the water on the floor — then with them over his shoulder and the timepiece in his hand, he found his direction for the hall and went upstairs, knowing the position of the 'observatory' from long familiarity. He had scarcely put down the furs and clock before he felt the house quake under a sudden, soundless impact. It did not dawn on him immediately what it might be. When it did he swung round in horror in the blackness and blundered to the stairs.

Hurrying down them he found his worst fears almost immediately realised. He was up to his waist in water, the pressure of it striving to drag him down.

He held on to the banister, cursing the silence and the dark. No use calling to Linda; no use listening for her own cries if she were still there. No use doing anything except feeling around in the flood that had evidently blasted clean through the neighbourhood.

He still held the banister and went lower down until the water was surging round his shoulders — but at this level, for his height was considerably above average, he was standing on the hall floor. If the water didn't get any higher for the next few minutes he would have time to investigate.

Floundering along as best he could, gripping the hall wall projections to save himself being bowled over, he managed to reach the kitchen doorway. Here the water was a torrent and he could imagine the din it must be making as it raced through the narrow space into the back garden. If only he could shout, or see!

Damn the blackness! Damn the Silence! He barked his knees on the cooker, which was still holding its own, and cursed still more to himself.

He gripped it for safety and felt along it, staring into the abyss; then it occurred to him that his hand was holding something that certainly was not metal. It moved quickly in his grasp. It was a Wellington boot. Therefore it must be on Linda's foot.

It was. In a second or two she was tapping him on the shoulder in a communication.

'Sheer blind luck you found me. I jumped up here out of the water — I've lost all the food.'

Holt tapped the answer back on her leg. 'Climb on my shoulders — piggyback — and we'll get out of here. Upstairs is our only chance and I am tall enough to keep my head above water.'

Linda asked no questions: she simply did as she was told. The moment she was firmly settled Holt started back on the return journey, making every step with difficulty against the onrushing waters. They were rising higher, too. Several times before he groped for and found the staircase he found his mouth and nose submerged and emerged again spluttering for breath. Added to this was the fact that the water was icily cold. Though it had thawed out it had not had the time to heat up.

The staircase! Holt found it at last and grabbed the banister. After that it was easy. Step by step, Linda perched in the blackness on his shoulders, he made his way upwards, finally depositing her on her feet when he reached the upper landing. Together they made their way into the observatory and Holt closed the door.

Linda's hand reached out to him. It was cold and wet.

'How did you know what had happened? No sounds, or anything!'

'I felt the impact when the water hit the house — I've got to get these wet things off and wrap myself in the furs. How about you?'

'Only dampened — nothing worse. I'll dry off.'

Holt moved away and for the next ten minutes he was busy changing his clothes. Then he felt around again and discovered that Linda had seated herself on the old-fashioned couch that lay near the telescope — chiefly to facilitate looking through the instrument without severe craning of the head.

'Food went, you say?' Holt's fingers tapped gently on Linda's forearm.

'Yes. I thought only of saving myself. What do we do?'

'I just don't know.'

Long pause; then Holt made a further observation: 'We ate quite recently, thank goodness, so that should keep us going for awhile. After that we'll just have to hope for the best. If only the everlasting night would lift! It would solve everything at one stroke!'

'You still think that it will?'

'I'm more certain of it now than I have been all along. The return of heat radiations makes it logical that everything else, including sound, should make its return.'

'How soon?'

'That's the point! It depends on whether it will be soon enough. We are in a particularly difficult position with no food to sustain us and floods in all directions. We'll have water, anyway. and that's something. We will be able to survive longer without food than we could without water.'

Linda made no response. They were back again on the old, nerve-shattering game of waiting — and waiting, but in this they were no different from tens of thousands of other men and women throughout the world, most of them not having the least scientific knowledge of what had happened, or what could still happen.

One in a hundred perhaps understood that the return of heat radiations, emanated even from the invisible sun, meant that part of the barrier had broken down, but strangely enough they did not see in this happening a possible precursor to the resumption of light and sound. What all of them *did* understand, with painful realism, was that they were in the midst of floods and fighting for their lives.

The North London projector site, where Luther and his men had decided to await the end, was no exception from the ravaging waters that had inundated the Rankin home. The site was swept away in a tidal wave in which three of the engineers were drowned whilst Luther and two other men — lost to him in the darkness — survived. Luther, as near as he could tell, when the waters seemed to have reached a fixed level, was perched on the roof of some kind of building to which he had clung after being carried several miles by the flood.

Absorbing the miracle that he was still alive he began to investigate the situation, ultimately finding his exploring fingers gripping a roof trapdoor. It required considerable nerve to find there was darkness below it and a ladder leading into the unknown, but Luther descended the ladder just the same and then tried to imagine where he was. From the feel of things he was surrounded by metallic walls and objects. The more he explored the more certain became that he was in some kind of powerhouse . . .

Powerhouse! Of course, why not? The North London powerhouse, from which several of the projectors had taken their power, was a great isolated building two or three miles distant from the city proper. There was nothing unusual in the fact that the flood had swept him straight to it because if was the only building in the track of the waters until London itself was reached.

With added urgency Luther continued his investigations. As a scientist he had gathered long ago that since heat radiations had returned radio waves must also have done so. Get power going and radio apparatus could work too — not for the purpose of sound or light transmission, obviously, but for remote control of machines which might help to sort out the rightful chaos which had descended upon the planet. Also it might be possible somehow to restore power to the remaining two North London projectors if they had escaped the flood.

Altogether Luther was full of good intentions, but limited by the relentless circumstances of the moment. Ten minutes later his bright ideas crumbled as he found, on struggling in the dark to the ground floor of the great building, that it was five feet under water. No return of power was possible under such circumstances, even if he could ever find his way to the vital switchboards.

He sighed and stared blindly around him in the darkness. And it was as he stood there that he wondered if perhaps the strain of events was at last proving too much for him. For he was sure he could hear something. It was infinitely far away, certainly — or appeared to be — like something heard on a radio with the volume control turned down to minimum. It was a curious sort of sound, rather like voices on the astral plane with a background very much like that of water running over stones.

Luther frowned to himself. Obviously the sounds must be in his head. Had not the medical faculty said that ears, so long unused during the Silence, would never function again even if sound returned? *Was* sound returning? Did those strange voices, quite unintelligible, really exist or were they in some other dimension? No place where they *could* exist in a powerhouse, was there?

Luther did not try and answer his own

hazy questions. He got on the move instead, drawn by the magic of sound in the Silence, but the voices' location still evaded him. Somewhere overhead. That was where they seemed to be.

A thought struck him. The powerhouse, like all the great public utilities, was fitted — for normal times — with a radio loud-speaker left permanently in action and powered by almost everlasting batteries, independent of normal power supply.

The reason was so that the engineers could receive very urgent messages during an unexpected breakdown in power. In normal times, yes — but these were not normal times. Just the same there was no known reason why the radio should still not be functioning even though for a very long time no sound had come forth.

Luther twisted around in the swirling waters and clawed his way back to the ladder down which he had originally descended. He was still not sure whether the sounds were not in his head. Hastily he began climbing — too hastily for a man of his years and in blank darkness as well. At the top of the ladder he missed his grip, clawed outwards into space, and dropped the whole thirty-foot length back into the flood again.

The fall and the water he might possibly have survived, but not the blow on the back of the head from a nearby submerged generator. The tumbling waters surged onward and Luther went with them, the mystery which had intrigued him destined not to be solved this side of Eternity . . .

For Holt and Linda there were certainly no 'astral voices' or sounds of any sort. The only consolation they had was that they were reasonably warm, but it weighed little against the intolerable longing for sight and sound, a desire made all the more poignant because both of them felt such blessings were within measurable reach of fulfilment — yet still they did not manifest themselves. Had they had a radio in action they would have realised that sound was, in places, filtering through the slowly corroding barrier of the alien electrical force as the energy which had been blasted into it went still further in the complicated electronic process of finding a balance.

Yes, in odd spots of the planet sound was apparent, in places as far apart as the Arctic Circle and equatorial Africa. Radio waves were definitely re-established in full force all over the planet: they had returned at the same time as heat. Which meant that Luther had not heard 'astral voices' but a broadcast from Greenland, to which isolated and frozen land — even in normal times — sound had fully been restored. Being a land accustomed to ice and snow, the buildings thereon were made to stand it, which accounted for the fact that the radio station was unharmed. An excited announcer was doing his best to tell the world that the Silence was being broken — but few there were who heard him. And those who did, through some permanently 'on' set or others equipped with batteries, imagined they were going crazy.

And light? Nowhere on the face of the Earth was the darkness lifting. The most precious necessity of all was still missing. It left those who had the benefit of sound wondering which condition was the worst

— sound without light, or vice-versa.

In the 'observatory' Linda stirred herself from her lounging position on the floor to tap a question:

'What time is it, Holt?'

'Does it matter?'

'Of course it matters! As long as we're still alive we want to know how the time's going. At least I do.'

Holt felt around for the clock and fingered the face. It was just after six o'clock, of which fact he informed Linda and then relaxed again. Six o'clock, eight o'clock, midnight — what the devil did it matter, anyway, with nothing but everlasting night? With every second that passed Holt's eager anticipations were sinking again. The scientist in him kept insisting that if anything were going to happen it would have done so by now. Linda, on the other hand, unclouded by any such positive theories, was prepared to wait — and wait — and still wait.

'How long do you think we'll be able to hold out without food?' she questioned presently.

'A long time, with so much water

available. That's the main thing; and maybe we could kill the monotony a little, by getting some by us in readiness. I'll go down into the kitchen.'

'Then I'll come with you — '

Holt restrained the girl as he felt her rise beside him. His fingers tapped on her arm.

'No sense in your doing that. You're not tall enough to keep your chin over the flood, and I don't relish a second 'piggy-back'.'

With that he gave her an encouraging pat on the shoulder and then found his way to the door. In a few seconds he was cautiously descending the stairs, but to his surprise the lower he went there was no sign of the raging waters. Only when he actually got to the hall did he find any, brimming over his ankles. The only explanation could be that the waters had spent themselves or drained off into a myriad sewers, depressions and cavities in the landscape. What they had actually done was empty themselves in the North London Basin, the great reservoir north of the city close beside the powerhouse where Luther had fallen to his death.

Holt hesitated for a moment, wondering if he should tell Linda; then he changed his mind. In any case there could be no comfort down here with everything wringing wet: the only advantage lay in the fact that food could probably be found after all. Most of it had been tinned, and in the refrigerator — therefore anchored — so death by starvation might be circumvented after all.

He found the foods he wanted, loaded himself with them, and returned upstairs to explain. The result was that Linda came down with him the next time, and against the possibility of further devouring waters, they removed every conceivable thing they could possibly have a use for, including the radio set from the lounge together with the electric radiator, and took them into the observatory. If it did nothing else it found them something to do.

'All power will be off, won't it?' Linda's signals asked. 'So where's the sense in the radio and radiator?'

'The sense in it is that since heat-radiations have returned, radio waves

— including those used for broadcasting — must have done so as well. Also, since the floods had dropped there is a reasonable chance that any surviving engineers may do their utmost to get the powerhouses running again. If that happens, the moment sound comes back — and I'm hoping it will — we want to be in touch with events.'

With that Holt began to flounder around again, searching for the power point in the skirting board. He rediscovered it finally and plugged the radio into it. It was that, or the heater, since he had no multi-point adaptor handy. The air was reasonably mild, though, so for the time being the radiator could be dispensed with. This done he made sure the radio was reasonably dry, which it was, chiefly because it was of the modern 'high-level' variety, originally fixed nearly at the height of the ceiling. Such sets were common, chiefly to save space in small rooms, and in this instance it had placed the apparatus just clear of the floodwaters.

'So far, so good,' Holt signalled, when the simple task was finished. 'Maybe we'd better get something to eat once again — I've just remembered that there's a paraffin stove in the outhouse, the one we use in frosty weather. If it could be used we could have hot drinks. There's a drum of paraffin there too.'

'Too dangerous,' was Linda's response. 'If we knocked the stove over we'd have the place on fire in a moment and not be able to see it. We'd better stick to water.'

They did — un-boiled and generally filthy flood water, which they had brought up in several jugs. Certainly it was out of the cold water tap, but the floods had so polluted the normal supply it tasted like stale cauliflower juice.

They ate and drank nevertheless, the tinned food awkwardly opened in the dark with the key supplied for the purpose. They had just made an end of their cold and decidedly unpalatable repast when both of them were held for a second or two in frozen amazement by a deep-toned chiming only a few feet away from them!

Seven mellow strokes, perfectly clear and resonant, and as they died away they were replaced by a steady tick-tock, tick-tock, tick-tock . . .

Instantly Linda felt for Holt's hand in the darkness, to start signalling, then just as quickly she spoke instead — cautiously, half-afraid, and became almost instantly quiet again, queerly shocked.

'Holt, was — '

'Sound!' he whispered in ecstasy. 'Sound, Lin! It's come back! The Silence has gone! Listen — '

They listened as they never had in their lives before. There was the ticking clock, the sound of their own slight movements, the whispering of the wind outside, and their own slow, tense breathing.

Then Holt scrambled to his feet with what seemed a terrific amount of noise and found his way to the window. He fumbled with the catches and then flung the frame open wide. It was magnificent, glorious, to hear the sound of water surging in the distance, the stirring of leaf-denuded tree branches in the garden outside. These were the sounds of life, of hope — but as yet there were no other noises. No blurred undertone of traffic on the highway, no remoter bass from the metropolis. Children playing, dogs barking, neighbours hammering . . . These background essentials were still absent. It felt up here, in the observatory, as though it were the last outpost on a dead planet.

'Nothing doing?' Linda asked, coming to Holt's side.

He thought for a moment how wonderful it was to have been able to hear her approach; how even more wonderful to hear her voice.

'Nothing exceptional anyway,' he answered her. 'We must give it time. The restoration of sound will be such a miracle to most people it will take them a little while to get used to it. We can't expect anything really wonderful until this damnable darkness lifts also.'

'Seems more or less certain now that it will, doesn't it? Sound and heat and radio waves are back. Light must follow. It must.'

'Certainly the dyno-depressant field must be losing its influence,' Holt agreed. 'All a matter of that balance of forces I mentioned. When the two like charges are equal, and opposite, the whole thing must inevitably cancel out — and maybe with a God-awful thunderclap, too.'

'But can that happen when the charge you induced into the D-D field was so much less than the field itself?'

'Certainly. I thought I'd already explained that it is not necessary to upset the *whole* field. Unbalance even a part of it and the whole thing becomes unstable and evaporates — rather like a whisker of wire carrying a low current can short circuit a high-tension wire of thousands of volts.'

For a while Linda was silent in the darkness, gazing into it blindly and listening, her arm about Holt's fur-coated waist.

'Didn't the medical faculty say that we'd never hear again?' she asked at length. 'Something about unused organs?'

For the first time in weeks Holt laughed softly. 'And didn't I say they were crazy? That it takes years of disuse to make an organ fall into permanent disuse? Can't blame them: they diagnosed things from a medical standpoint whereas I viewed it from the scientific angle. One thing *is* possible, which may have misled them, namely, that under continued silence an ear closes up like a field daisy before a shower of rain. That fact was proven during experiments on potential airmen way back in the nineteen-fifties when tests were made to see what a total blackout of sound did to the human frame. It is quite likely that human ears closed up under the Silence, which fact the doctors observed before the dark descended — and they were led to the wrong conclusion. None of which matters! We can hear again.'

'And it's getting draughty with the window open!'

'Sorry, Lin. I've got furs on and hadn't noticed.' Holt felt around, closed the window once more, and holding Linda to him they returned to the sofa and sat upon it, still marvelling at the fact that sound was exactly as it had ever been. Whatever had been neutralising the action of the sound-particles had gone — they hoped forever.

Sound, in fact, had by now returned to all parts of the world and though the cowed millions of inhabitants were grateful for the passing of the Silence they were still under the crushing handicap of the total blackness. Those who did not know whether it would ever lift or not were at least courageous enough to believe that it could perhaps be circumvented now normal speech and communication were possible.

It caused a tremendous stirring amongst those who had so far survived. They began to make the effort, to emerge from their hundred and one 'foxholes', determined to talk to others, and with them, devise some means of getting things going again despite the still immensely difficult conditions. It was for this reason that engineers thought first of the powerhouses, the nerve-centres of everyday life, and set off into the blackness to see what they could do. Those already in the powerhouses had died from the cold, and some of them from the flood, but there still remained the relief staffs, who in the interval, had been 'sheltering' as best they could from the worst storm of elemental forces ever to betide Mankind.

The efforts of the engineers, not only in England, but in every country in the world, were worthy of the highest praise.

They worked every waking hour after the return of sound, in constant touch by walkie-talkie radio-apparatus, feeling their way through the abyss and commencing the immense task of drying out those vital parts of electrical equipment that had been affected by water. This was not the case in every instance, so in many cases the powerhouses were finally started up again twelve hours after sound had returned, which, by time, meant in the early hours of the following day.

The resumption of four powerhouses in Britain meant that thousands of homes could have electrical warmth again, even if it could not be seen. Radio stations were linked up, and for the first time since the catastrophe messages in a widely distributed scale began to come through — and Holt and Linda, having awakened disconsolately to discover the eternal night was still there, were amongst those who found their radio set in action. Reception was bad owing to low power, but it had the virtue of being intelligible.

So, as they ate their unappetising breakfast and swilled it down with the filthy-tasting water, Holt and Linda began to grasp in some measure the extent of the catastrophe that had hit the world. There were no death-rolls as yet because the still unrelieved darkness made an assessment impossible, but it was believed from the fragmentary reports coming in that millions — literally millions — of human beings had been wiped out, chiefly by the deadly cold or else the floods. The worst hit areas, as far as the cold was concerned, had been the tropic regions. The hapless people inhabiting these regions had simply wilted under the below zero temperatures, the Silence, and the Dark.

Because of the Dark it was impossible to say whether the 'Holt Rankin Project', only half completed before disaster had overtaken it, had been a success or not. Nobody, it appeared, was willing to concede to Holt the glory of having brought back warmth and sound to the stricken world. The general assumption seemed to be that the alien electrical field had somehow done it of its own accord, an observation which made Holt smile wryly to himself in the blackness as the news bulletin — which the announcer had apparently memorised from radio reports, or else 'read' it from Braille copy — came to an end with the promise of a further one in a few hours.

''Blow, blow, thou winter wind, thou art not so unkind as man's ingratitude','' Holt murmured, and gave a sigh. 'Y'know, Lin, I have the feeling that if we ever do emerge completely from this mess I'm not going to be half the hero I somehow expected I'd be.'

'They make me sick!' Linda retorted. 'Because they know your *entire* project didn't succeed they can't credit that half of it did.'

'Maybe it hasn't,' Holt answered, suddenly gloomy again. 'If the darkness doesn't lift we can't call ourselves so much better off after all. A world of blind inhabitants won't be much use, will it?'

'I don't really know,' Linda's voice was quiet. 'For myself I've become so accustomed to the darkness I do believe I could carry on for the rest of my life amidst it — and amount to something as well.

Blind folks have done it for generations. What is the difference between localised and general blindness?'

'The difference is that in normal conditions there are sighted people to help the blind. In the present conditions, with nobody able to see, I just can't imagine how we'd stand it. I don't pretend that I could. I'd sooner be dead.'

Again Linda was silent, then: 'Did you ever read Wells's 'Country of the Blind'? There was a good example of how a sightless community can exist. After all, if *everybody* is bereft of what is considered one of the most vital faculties Nature must surely atone in some way? She'd provide us with sharper hearing, more sensitive touch, keener instincts. But why do I talk this way?' Linda broke off. 'The light will return because it must.'

'Just the same,' Holt commented, 'I think we'd be more sensible if we planned for the possible non-return of light. For myself my whole life and career is based on light and the necessity of seeing. Without sight I'm finished and don't want to go on living. In fact,' he finished slowly, 'If the light has not returned by the time our present provisions have given out I'm going to put a stop to things for myself.'

'Put — a stop?' There was a chill round Linda's heart.

'Yes — because it's better than dying of starvation, which we certainly will after the provisions have gone. How do you suppose we can ever find our way to the food depots? How do we know the food depots are even there after the floods?'

'We don't, of course. I'm hoping that the Government has arranged something since sound has returned — some way for all people to reach the food warehouses.'

'If there is a Government any more. Those who comprised it may be as dead as many millions of other folks, as well as the blind people who had charge of the depots.'

Silence for a while, then: 'Holt, your attitude is so suddenly pessimistic it's got me guessing — and worried. It would not be caused by the fact that the world has ignored what you have done to try and save it, would it?'

'Might be. I'm not anxious to carry on under impossible conditions amongst a people who haven't a spark of gratitude.'

Linda said nothing. She could hardly blame Holt for his attitude. An embittered man will do anything, and he was no exception.

'But if all goes well?' she ventured.

'I can afford to forget the lack of appreciation — or else I'll spend a good deal of my time proving that the D-D could not have collapsed except for my idea. I'm not being egotistical about the thing, Lin. It's a matter of prestige. If things go right I'll return to being chief of the physics department, of course, but I'll stay in that position for the rest of my life unless I do something worthy of promotion. My counteractive system to the dyno-depressant is enough in itself to give me the boost I need, which is why I've got to justify myself. Maybe Luther will stand by me — if he's still alive.'

'And if it stays dark you mean to put yourself out when the provisions are finished?'

Long pause then Holt murmured a

quiet 'Yes — And you'd have sound common sense if you agreed to end it with me. Forget all those silly ideas about mastering the difficulties. They can't be mastered when everybody is in the same boat. You know what it says about the blind leading the blind.'

The clock struck nine deliberately. Nine in the morning. Black as the lowest regions of hell. Linda sat thinking. She could hear Holt breathing close beside her, could almost sense that his face was turned towards her, as though watching her. Go on alone if he carried out his threat? She shook her head to herself. Ideals about courage were one thing: facing up to merciless fact was another.

'What would you suggest to — to finish things?' she asked.

'There are sleeping tablets in the bedroom, hangovers of when I was so ill. Half a bottle of them if I remember rightly. Divide those between us at one go and that's the finish.'

'But — ' Linda stirred uncomfortably. 'But, Holt, isn't that extremely drastic? Wouldn't it be better to hold out to the last gasp on the chance the Dark may pass?'

'I don't think so. The provisions we have should last a week. If the darkness hasn't lifted by then I think we can consider it reasonably certain that it is not going to — that the best the energy we released could do was alleviate the sound and warmth radiations, but not light — '

'Then isn't it a matter of getting the projectors to work again to finish the job?'

'Scattered as they now must be, the original engineers all lost, and the darkness hampering everything? No, Lin, the Project, whatever the outcome, is dead.'

Linda seemed to be thinking, then presently she said; 'I suppose I'm crazy, but I can think of a reason why light is longer delayed in its return than anything else.'

'Well?'

'Because it isn't just one radiation, but several! It's a combination of the colours added together, isn't it, the combined effect of which makes white light?'

'That's right.'

'Then maybe with so many radiations involved it is taking a longer time to achieve the balance, or whatever it is.'

'Possible,' Holt admitted, clearly interested in the speculation, but he did not pursue it further. He had made his decision, apparently, and meant to abide by it.

So the gruelling, grim monotony resumed — the round of eating, drinking, sleeping, and listening to the radio reports with their tale of woe. And still the darkness did not lift, nor was there any report of it doing so in the radio bulletins.

On the seventh day Linda found her hands groping at one tin of provisions. The remainder had gone. She did not say anything for fear of what Holt would do — but evidently he had investigated for himself, for when the meal was over he said briefly:

'That was the last one, wasn't it?'

'Well, yes, it was, but — '

'No buts about it as far as I'm concerned, Lin. I've had enough. Tell me straight: how do you feel about it?'

'I don't quite know. I'd go on struggling if you were there too; otherwise I couldn't face it.'

'Darkness is here to stay; that is what I believe now,' Holt said harshly. 'It's a damnable thing, I know, to have half succeeded and been cheated of the remainder — '

'Unless, there being so many radiations — '

'That, too, I find hard to credit any more. Here — ' There was a clink and Holt's rasping breathing: 'Give me your hand. There's a small heap of sleeping tablets for you, and the same for me. Now, I fill up the cups with this stinking water, so — ' There was the sound of his action and then he said quietly: 'Believe me, Lin, it will be better than starving to death, forgotten, damned, in rayless night. There must be something better beyond this abyss.'

Linda took the tablets and could feel herself shaking with the intensity of the moment. Then Holt grasped her shoulder and began to pilot her around.

'We've lived together, dearest,' he murmured, kissing her gently, 'so let's start on the new journey the same way. Take the inside of the sofa. I'll take the outside, using the two chairs to extend it. There, that's it.'

Even though she half wondered why she complied so meekly, Linda nonetheless obeyed, lying flat on her back on the sofa, the sleeping tablets in her clenched right hand. Holt was busy for a while in the blackness and then he settled, likewise on his back, beside her.

'We could do worse than try a prayer,' he murmured. 'Might help us on our way. Something short, like: 'God, the Father of us all, we commend our spirits to Thee, who made us out of Thine own infinite wisdom and goodness. Amen'.'

'Amen,' Linda whispered, weeping silently to herself.

Holt moved again, then he took her left hand and placed a cup of water in it.

'Don't spill,' he murmured. 'Or does it matter? Drink when I do. May as well have some sort of system, even in this.'

He raised his own cup, the pills in his hand, and then to Linda's surprise he suddenly gave a gasp of anguish, starting so violently he upset his cup of water upon her.

'What in the world — !' she gasped.

'God!' he whispered. 'Oh, my God! I *saw* something. It went through my eye like a knife — Wait a minute! Where the devil was it — ?'

He shifted and turned in the blackness, keeping his eyes half shut this time, then suddenly that searing spot was right in front of him again, glowing with the intensity of molten steel. His eyes, the right one, so long deadened with the dark, just could not adjust itself without intense pain — but he hung on, sweating, wondering, staring with slowly accustoming retina at this miracle.

A star! No, thousands of stars with one intense one in the midst . . .

'*Light!*' he nearly screamed. 'The stars! They're shining again — It's the telescope I'm looking through, poised right over this sofa — Don't eat those tablets — '

Linda dimly grasped that he had looked accidentally right into the eyepiece directly overhead and seen the starry heavens. Now he was floundering around to the window. There was a click as he flung it wide . . .

'Quickly!' he shouted. 'Come! Come and look!'

Linda was already off the sofa, pills and suicide-pact forgotten. She hurried to Holt's side, her own eyes starting to twinge as she stared into a heaven dusted from end to end with stars and nebulae, just as it had always been — though down on the Earth's surface there was still that awful gloom.

'It's going!' Holt exulted. 'The D-D's beaten! What time is it? Yes — ten in the morning. Soon the clearance will have spread to the sun and — '

He stopped. A dim suggestion of deepest violet was creeping into the awful dark. It suffused it slowly, and high in the starry sky a translucent circle of heliotrope began to make itself apparent. Imperceptibly it changed to indigo, and with it the circle became a tangible ball that struck straight into the roots of the brain of those watching it.

Tortured after the deadly blackness Linda and Holt both jerked their heads away from the returning lord of day.

But around them they saw seas of indigo swirl off into molten sapphire in which their surroundings began to dance with joyous, radiant waves.

Green, sickly as the depths of the ocean . . . Yellow, bright as the marigold, and with it the stars paled and the black sky became faintly blue . . .

Orange, and the light was intensifying. Red, like the malignant sunset of hardest winter . . . Then the red faded before the full-born effulgence of the natural photosphere and the blinding sun poured down daylight on this western hemisphere, destroying every shadow, wiping out the dark, drenching the muddy, wrecked countryside in steamy radiance.

Holt could not speak; his emotions were too great. He only realised that he was holding the weeping, half-laughing Linda in his arms whilst both of them forced their aching eyes to accustom once more to the glory of a newborn day.

THE END

CLIMATE INCORPORATED
THE FIVE MATCHBOXES
EXCEPT FOR ONE THING
BLACK MARIA, M.A.
ONE STEP TOO FAR
THE THIRTY-FIRST OF JUNE
THE FROZEN LIMIT
ONE REMAINED SEATED
THE MURDERED SCHOOLGIRL
SECRET OF THE RING
OTHER EYES WATCHING
I SPY . . .
FOOL'S PARADISE
DON'T TOUCH ME
THE FOURTH DOOR
THE SPIKED BOY
THE SLITHERERS
MAN OF TWO WORLDS
THE ATLANTIC TUNNEL
THE EMPTY COFFINS
LIQUID DEATH
PATTERN OF MURDER
NEBULA
THE LIE DESTROYER
PRISONER OF TIME

MIRACLE MAN
THE MULTI-MAN
THE RED INSECTS
THE GOLD OF AKADA
RETURN TO AKADA
GLIMPSE
ENDLESS DAY
THE G-BOMB
A THING OF THE PAST
THE BLACK TERROR